P9-CRI-705

Creative
Woman
MYSTERIES

ℱ Deadly Stitch

Susan Sleeman

Annie's®
AnniesFiction.com

Books in the Creative Woman Mysteries series

A Deadly Stitch
Copyright © 2022 Annie's.

All rights reserved. No part of this publication may be reproduced, stored in a retrieval system, or transmitted in any form or by any means—electronic, mechanical, photo-copying, recording or otherwise—without the prior written permission of the publisher. The only exception is brief quotations in printed reviews. For information address Annie's, 306 East Parr Road, Berne, Indiana 46711-1138.

The characters and events in this book are fictional, and any resemblance to actual persons or events is coincidental.

Library of Congress-in-Publication Data
A Deadly Stitch / by Susan Sleeman
p. cm.
I. Title
                 2022933537

AnniesFiction.com
800-282-6643
Creative Woman Mysteries®
Series Editor: Shari Lohner

10 11 12 13 14 | Printed in China | 9 8 7 6 5 4 3 2 1

— I —

The weather turned out perfect for Dedication Day—sunny, with bright blue skies and a cool, Oregon breeze.

Rows of chairs set up on the side lawn of the Paisley Craft Market & Artist Lofts began to fill up as its proud owner, Shannon McClain, took her place behind the podium. *What a glorious day for a celebration.* She'd hired a vocal group to entertain and a few local vendors to serve up refreshments to the eager crowd.

Shannon tapped the microphone once to test it. The ping reverberated, proving it was hot. Gazing out across the audience, she saw many familiar faces. Her mother, Beth, with whom she'd recently been reunited after thirty-six years, sat in a chair in the very front row. Behind her were the members of the Purls of Hope knitting circle. Shannon smiled at them, overwhelmed with the kinship she now felt toward these new friends. Betty, a proud grandmother and staunch Jane Austen fan, sat on the aisle. Next to her was Joyce, the owner of the Pink Sprinkles Bakery. With her chic, platinum bob and hot pink lipstick, Joyce was a stand-out in any crowd. Kate, the youngest of their knitting group and owner of Ultimutt Grooming, wrestled with the Beagle pup in her lap—the newest stray to land on her doorstep. And who could forget Melanie, the woman who had taught them all a lesson in courage and strength during her recent battle with breast cancer.

Chief Grayson and a deputy were there as well, lingering near the back of the crowd. But there was one face in particular Shannon didn't see.

Michael Stone.

She cleared her throat and began: "As those of you who are familiar with me know, I come from a small coastal town in Scotland. It's a place filled with people who are proud of their traditions, people who are warm and friendly and love their families. They are a people much like the gracious and wonderful population of Apple Grove, Oregon, my newly adopted home."

A few claps sounded, then faded as she resumed her speech.

"It's easy to see why my grandmother loved living here. Today, in the spirit of Victoria's generous heart, I wish to continue her legacy of charitable contribution."

The crowd erupted into full-blown applause. She noticed that the Purls clapped louder and longer than anyone else. Betty even put her thumb and index finger in her mouth and let out a long whistle.

"To do so, we will sacrifice part of our stockroom and all of the garden landscaping around the Paisley Craft Market & Artist Lofts in order to launch Espresso Yourself, a public coffeehouse and workroom space dedicated to craft groups who come together to create, display, and sell items to raise money for charitable organizations."

She paused as she noticed a familiar stride. Michael approached the crowd and stood near the back. He nodded when she spotted him.

Shannon swallowed hard. "And now, without further ado, I will attempt to break ground."

As had been prearranged her store manager, Essie Engleman, approached the podium bearing a yellow hard hat and a shovel. Shannon donned the hat and chose a spot in the middle of the garden. Determined to dig out an impressive chunk rather than the ceremonial shovelful, she plunged the shiny new shovel deep into the soil, hoisted the dirt, and tossed it aside.

The crowd clapped again, and she signaled to the man waiting with a backhoe to proceed.

She moved a few steps out of his way as he began to dig and turned to face her friends, a triumphant smile on her face. The applause began to dwindle, and a few people in the front row stood up to point at something behind her.

Shannon turned to look as the backhoe ground to a halt. A blue tarp stuck up from the dirt, wrapped around a large object.

Quickly, Michael pushed through the crowd and stood next to her for a moment before crouching down for a better look. Worry clouded his blue eyes.

Chief Grayson joined them. "What is it, Stone?"

"Judging by the smell ..." He pulled a handkerchief from his coat and held it to his nose, then pulled a section of the tarp away. "... it's a body."

Grayson looked over Stone's shoulder. He lifted his cap up from his forehead. "Oh boy." He pulled the radio off his duty belt and began to issue orders.

Shannon stared in disbelief. "Do you know who it is?"

A woman behind her screamed. Shannon whirled to find Melanie standing there, staring at the body.

"No, no, no!" she shouted.

Joyce and Kate rushed to Melanie's side just as her face turned ghostly white and her legs gave out.

"Come on," Betty said. "Let's get her away from here." Joyce and Kate helped Betty move Melanie to the other side of the street.

"I know who it is." Grayson knelt down next to Michael. "It's Edward Burkhart, Melanie's ex-husband."

Shannon's heart thundered in her chest as she stared at Edward's body. Something metallic protruded from his neck. It caught the sun and sent up a piercing light. "Och! There's a knitting needle stuck in his neck! And is that yarn? His wrists are tied with yarn?"

Before she could utter another word, Chief Grayson came to his feet, blocking her view of the body. "I'm not ready for everyone in town to hear these details, Shannon, so I'd appreciate it if you'd stop yelling," he said.

Yelling? She hadn't been yelling.

Or had she?

The chief shooed the crowd across the street and away from the Paisley Craft Market. Their gaping mouths and frenzied whispers, coupled with Michael's narrowed eyes, told her the chief was right. She *had* been yelling. But she couldn't help it.

There's a dead body in my lawn!

"Stay there," the chief instructed Shannon. Then he rushed over to Melanie and engaged her in conversation. After a few minutes, he marched back toward Shannon's side of the street, barking orders at his men on the way.

Shannon felt oddly detached from the chaotic activities unfolding like a blurry dream around her. Only it wasn't a dream. Edward Burkhart *had* been murdered. *Who would commit such a heinous crime? And had the killer hoped Edward would be unearthed at today's ceremony ... or was that purely coincidence?*

The chief joined Shannon, and as she opened her mouth to ask his opinion, sirens cut through the air, spiraling ever closer. He turned away from her to face the ambulance. Blue lights twisting, the vehicle raced down Apple Grove's Main Street, past the antique street lamps and quaint shops. It slowed as it approached Shannon's craft market.

"That'll be for Melanie," the chief said matter-of-factly.

Melanie! In her momentary state of shock, Shannon had forgotten about her friend. She whirled and scanned the whispering crowd, searching for Melanie. Relief washed over her when she spotted her seated on the curb, fully conscious. Melanie sat sandwiched between Kate and Betty. Joyce stood next to them, her arms crossed over her red fleece pullover, the jeweled zipper pull glinting in the sun.

Melanie suddenly looked up. Her green eyes, usually so soft and trusting, were filled with grief.

"I need to go to Melanie." Shannon started toward her friend but the chief grabbed her arm and ground her steps to a halt.

"I asked you to stay here, remember?"

Shannon took deep breaths of the salty sea air, trying to clear her head and remember everything the chief had said since the gruesome discovery. He'd fired off instructions like a drill sergeant, directing people away from the body, kneeling next to Melanie and questioning her while his men stood sentry. Then he'd come back to Shannon and, yes, he *had* mentioned something about keeping Melanie separated from her. But why?

"I need to finish securing the scene," the chief said, sharing a knowing look with Michael. "Would you mind ...?"

"I'll look after her." Michael moved closer to Shannon, assuming the protector role he'd taken since she'd first arrived in Apple Grove.

Shannon started to protest; she was a grown woman who did not require "looking after." But then she decided it might not be a bad thing to have Michael at her side. As a former Portland police detective, and co-owner of Stone & McCrary Security Consultants, he could explain what was happening and answer her questions.

"Here you go, Chief." Officer Steve Brownley handed the chief a thick roll of yellow tape.

"I'll get back to you as soon as possible, Shannon." The chief took the crime scene tape and tied one end to a tall stake Brownley had pounded into the ground. He kept unrolling the tape as he walked backward, his head bent and focused on his work, until he'd not only traveled the length of the garden, but past the Paisley Craft Market as well. He secured the tape on another post and moved on, turning the corner. The plastic strip fluttered in the wind, dancing and dipping like the kites children flew along the beach—just a few short miles away.

Shannon shivered. *This can't be happening. Not here. Not today of all days.*

"Hey," Michael said, slipping out of his jacket. "Everything will be OK." He draped his suit coat over her shoulders.

The unexpected compassion in his piercing blue eyes

was nearly her undoing. The tears she'd managed to hold back threatened to fall. She looked away before they did and saw the medic drop a silver blanket over Melanie's deflated shoulders.

Shannon turned back to Michael and met his questioning gaze. "I'm really worried about Melanie," she said. "I want to go over there and give her a big hug, but the chief said something about keeping us separated. Does that make sense to you?"

Michael nodded. "Melanie is the victim's former spouse. As such, Grayson has to consider the possibility she might somehow be involved in his death."

"But that's crazy! How could he entertain such a thought?"

"It's nothing personal against Melanie," Michael reassured her. "Grayson's following standard procedure. Also, since the body was found on your property, I expect he'll ask if you aided her in disposing of it."

Shannon felt her jaw drop. "If I *aided* her? I had nothing to do with this. How could you possibly think—"

"Whoa." Michael held up his hands in surrender. "*I* know you're not involved, but the chief has a job to do. That means keeping you away from Melanie so you can't discuss the case until after he speaks with both of you."

Shannon felt her anger rise. "He's already talked to Melanie," she snapped.

"Right. That means she's told him she had nothing to do with Edward's death," Michael replied, his voice calm. "You do the same thing, and then your part in this will be over."

Over. That sounded good. Shannon sighed and looked

up at him. "Thanks for the explanation. I knew there was a reason you were good to have around."

"Being a former cop does have its advantages. Wait until you lock yourself out of that old pickup your grandmother left you. I'll have you back inside in a flash." He smiled at her with that crooked little grin she'd seen in the rare moments he let his guard down.

A loud disturbance sounded across the road, and his grin vanished. Shannon turned and spotted the chief shouldering his way through the crowd, warning people to go home. He carried himself with authority, and his brown eyes held the same no-nonsense glint as before. He had a reputation for being a tough, by-the-book kind of guy. Being interviewed by him was not going to be pleasant.

"I guess he's coming to question me," Shannon muttered, turning back to Michael.

He watched her in silence, his usual dark and brooding expression firmly back in place. Shannon knew something troubled him. It was there, lurking in his eyes, most of the time.

"Michael?" she asked, as she shifted his coat on her shoulders, inhaling the minty scent of his soap.

He looked away and ran a hand through his dark hair. "Tell Grayson the truth, and you'll be fine."

"I don't suppose you could stay with me?" She hated how weak she sounded, but she'd never had to deal with a murder investigation before.

"I'm afraid not. Grayson will insist on talking with you in private."

The chief paused and glanced back at the building. He

offered a warning look to the young officer he'd left behind. The chief rarely let anything—even a parking ticket—escape his purview. Allowing one of his men to stand guard at a homicide scene had to be a big test for the younger man.

"C'mon, people. Move along," the chief commanded, issuing stern looks and crinkling a face that already held a road map of wrinkles as he marched toward Shannon. "There's nothing to see here."

"Call me if you need my help," Michael said.

"Don't forget this." Shannon shrugged out of his jacket and handed it to him. After a quick wave to the chief, Michael strode away.

Feeling alone and vulnerable, Shannon wrapped her arms around her stomach and swallowed her unease.

"Thanks for waiting." The chief stopped directly in front of her, his close proximity invading her personal space.

Instinctively, Shannon stepped back. "What can I do to help, Chief Grayson?" She kept her voice as pleasant as possible.

He lifted his cap and wiped a hand over his sweaty forehead. "Enough of this chief business. My friends all call me Grayson, and any friend of Michael's is a friend of mine."

"OK," she said, though she wasn't sure they could be friends if he actually thought she had anything to do with the dead body in her flower bed.

"I'm gonna get right to the point." Grayson settled the cap back on his balding head and fixed his focus on her. The intensity of his gaze was quite unsettling. "Do you have any idea why Ed would be buried on your property?"

"No. Of course not. In fact, I wanted to ask you the

same question." Shannon resisted the urge to fidget, not wanting to do anything that might make Grayson mistakenly think she was involved in the gruesome mess.

"If memory serves me correctly, Melanie and Ed had split up by the time you moved to Apple Grove," the chief said, pulling a notepad from his pocket.

"That's right. I'd never even met Edward." *And what a perfectly horrific way to meet him now.* "All I know about him is that he was married to Melanie, he left her when she got sick, and then he moved to Portland—where he was a helicopter pilot for a sightseeing tour company."

The chief jotted a quick note on his pad. "So he stayed in the same line of work as he'd been in here?"

"As far as I know. Melanie doesn't talk about him much."

"Do you have any thoughts on who might want to kill him? Other than Melanie, that is." He tipped his head toward Melanie, now seated on the rear bumper of the ambulance. She stretched her arm out so a medic could wrap a blood pressure cuff around it.

"Like I said," Shannon stated firmly. "I didn't even know Edward, so I don't have a clue who might have wanted him dead. But I *do* know Melanie didn't kill him."

Grayson's gaze locked on her like a guided missile, his eyes fierce and challenging. "See, here's the thing. Ed's still wearing his pricey watch, and his wallet is intact. So this doesn't look like some random mugging or burglary gone wrong. Nor does it strike me as a murder at the hands of a stranger. That leaves me to believe someone close to the deceased had a hand in his death. In this case, that could be Melanie."

Shannon shook her head. "She's not close to Edward

anymore. I know she hasn't spoken to him or seen him since their divorce was final."

"And you're basing that statement on what?"

"Things she's told me."

The chief scoffed, "But you don't have any actual proof?"

"How could I possibly prove *that*?" Shannon pointed an accusatory finger at his chest. "And speaking of proof, what evidence do you have that Melanie did kill Ed?"

The chief paused for a moment, as if to regroup. "Let's start over. You saw the knitting needle in Ed's neck. Can you give me any information about it—like the model, manufacturer, places where it's sold, etc.?"

Shannon shook her head and edged away from him. "I'd need a better look at the needle to be able to do that. And there's no way you're getting me close enough to the body to do so." Remembering how the needle looked, protruding from the soft flesh of Edward's neck, sent a tidal wave of nausea through her body.

"Don't worry," Grayson said. "I wouldn't ask you to do that. But as soon as the medical examiner releases the needle, I'll need you to take a good look at it."

She nodded absently, her focus now on Melanie. Shannon already knew from the quick look she'd gotten earlier of the visible end of the needle that it was part of an interchangeable circular needle. And she also knew Melanie owned a lovely set of stainless steel needles just like it. But so did a lot of other knitters in town, a fact Shannon feared Grayson would ignore in his haste to pin the murder on Melanie. She resolved to keep the information to herself until he forced it out of her.

"Is there anything else you can tell me?" Grayson demanded.

"Nothing that I can think of." Shannon was careful to keep her tone neutral. "Now, if you're through questioning me, I'd like to move Melanie into my shop and out of the curious view of all these people."

Grayson held up a hand. "I'm afraid I can't let you go inside."

Shannon's stomach filled with dread. "Why not?"

"I have reason to believe that Ed may have been killed there."

"W-what?" she stammered, certain he'd lost his mind. "Why would you think that?"

"I'm not at liberty to share those details. But trust me, your shop is looking good for the murder scene." Grayson glanced over at her store with a satisfied gleam in his eyes.

"That's impossible." Her tone shot up, drawing attention from people around her. "I'd know it if someone was killed in my store."

Grayson arched a brow. "Is that right? In my opinion, the only way you could be so certain of that is if you already knew the actual location where Ed was killed. Has Melanie confided in you?"

"You're twisting my words. I—"

"Not twisting. I'm trying to make you see that someone *could* have entered your business when it was closed and killed Edward."

Shannon recalled her arrival to the store earlier that morning to prepare for the dedication ceremony. True, things had been hectic, but nothing was amiss or out of place, other than a bit of construction debris. And she certainly would have noticed a pool of blood. "But I saw no signs of a break-in or struggle," she said.

"Melanie works part time for you now, right?" Grayson asked. "Doesn't she have a key?"

"Yes, but there wasn't even a hint of a disturbance. I would've noticed if anything had been out of place."

"That simply means the killer cleaned up the mess. But he—or *she*," he said, pausing as if trying to emphasize Melanie's guilt, "is sure to have left evidence behind. I want a state forensics team to process the place before you all go traipsing in there. You can have access to your store again once that's completed."

Shannon sighed. "And how long will that take?"

He shrugged. "Depends on how backlogged they are. Could be done in a day, or it could take a week or more before they can get someone out here."

Shannon didn't want to lose a week's worth of business, but she could see that it would be pointless to argue with Grayson. He didn't care if she suffered financially or if she and the ladies of the Purls of Hope knitting circle lost their weekly meeting sanctuary. He wanted to convict a killer—at any cost.

"I'll take Melanie to my house then," Shannon said.

He gave a clipped nod. "I'll stop by after the body's been picked up to see if you or Melanie have thought of anything else that might help us with the investigation."

Shannon tried not to scowl at him, but she couldn't help it. He was unfairly targeting her friend. It was clear he didn't care about Melanie. Based on his actions so far, it appeared he'd like nothing more than to be able to charge Melanie with the murder of her ex-husband—regardless of whether she was truly guilty or not.

2

Shannon raced down the street toward Essie. With her taste in wildly colorful clothes, it wasn't hard to spot the free-spirited manager of the Paisley Craft Market & Artist Lofts standing behind the store's refreshment table. As was to be expected after the gruesome turn the day had taken, there was no one waiting in line for a slice of celebratory cake.

Shannon sighed. She'd had such high hopes for the unveiling of her plans for the coffee shop addition—minus the dead body—and none of them had come to fruition.

But that couldn't be her main focus at the moment. She could work on building her business later. Helping Melanie was all that mattered now. And that meant getting Essie to clean up so she could take Melanie home.

As Shannon approached, she saw that Essie was staring off into the distance, fingering the edge of her lacy top as her flowing skirt caught the breeze and fluttered like a flag. When she noticed Shannon, she hurried to the side of the table to meet her. "I saw you talking with the chief. What's happening?" Essie asked, eyes wide.

Shannon looked around to make sure their conversation couldn't be overheard. Rumors about the closure of her shop would fly through town soon enough. She didn't need to be the one to start them. "Grayson has decided to cordon off both the garden *and* the shop."

"The shop?" Essie's voice rose in surprise. "But why?"

"He's just covering all of his bases," Shannon answered vaguely, trying not to worry her employee. "Could you see if one of the neighboring shops might let us store everything we lugged out here today? And if it's not too much trouble, would you take care of cleaning up? I'd like to spend some time with Melanie to make sure she's OK."

"Of course." Essie looked past Shannon to where Melanie sat. "I can't imagine how she must be feeling. I mean, I know they weren't close anymore, but still. To see her ex-husband looking like that must be awful. Tell her I'm thinking about her, OK?"

Shannon nodded. "Is there anything else we need to do right now?"

"I should probably call all the artists who lease space upstairs to tell them that their lofts will be off-limits until we reopen," Essie said. "I'm sure those who give classes and sell their work from their lofts won't be happy about it. Actually, I have my chalk class scheduled for tomorrow too. Do you think I should cancel it?"

"Unfortunately, yes. Is that all that needs doing today?"

"That's all I can think of."

"OK. You can reach me on my cell if you run into any problems this afternoon," Shannon said. "I'll call you when we're allowed to return to the building."

With a quick wave goodbye to her trusted employee, Shannon crossed the street to join Melanie and the rest of the ladies from their knitting group, The Purls of Hope. They all still hovered protectively around Melanie, as if to shield her from the grim reality of the situation.

Shannon knelt in front of her friend, not liking the look of Melanie's pale complexion. "You coping all right, Mel?"

"I hate to admit it," Melanie replied, her expression pensive, "but I was so angry at Ed for bailing on me after my cancer diagnosis, I wished something bad would happen to him to make him suffer too. But now that he's dead ... I feel so guilty about it. And I'm actually very sad."

"That's not surprising," Betty said, pushing her curly auburn hair off her face. "You were married for a long time."

Melanie turned to Betty. "True. I think I'm mostly sad for Greg. Edward may have been a jerk to me, but my son lost his dad today. I don't know how I'm going to break the news to him."

A picture of the worst day of Shannon's life flashed before her eyes. Her twin children's sobs and horrified expressions as she'd told them about John's accident were still as fresh in her memory now as on that terrible day.

Three years ago her dear friend Coleen had helped her cope with the loss of her husband, and Shannon could do the same thing for Melanie now. "I know how hard that's going to be, sweetie. I can go with you to talk to Greg if you'd like," Shannon said.

Joyce squatted next to Shannon. "I'll go too."

Betty and Kate vigorously nodded their willingness to help as well.

"You all would do that for me?" Melanie glanced at each of them, her eyes brimming with tears.

"Of course we will." Joyce took Melanie's hand. "You girls are like family to me. And families stick together."

"Why don't we all go inside the store and make a plan?"

Betty suggested. "I've had about all the curious stares I can take out here."

"Unfortunately, that's not an option," Shannon said. "Grayson thinks Edward might have been killed in the store."

"*What?*" Melanie asked.

"It's OK." Shannon squeezed her friend's knee. "I believe Grayson is wrong, and they won't find anything. However, we aren't allowed inside until they finish their investigation in and around the property."

"Are you sure nothing happened in there?" Melanie asked.

"I'm positive. Let's not give it another thought." Shannon sighed. "I could sure use a cup of coffee. What about you girls?"

The women all murmured their agreement.

Shannon stood and got the paramedic's attention. "Is it OK for Melanie to leave?"

"Yeah, she's fine." The medic peered down at Melanie. "Make sure you take it easy today."

Melanie nodded as she slipped out from under the blanket. The sudden temperature change made her tremble so Shannon shrugged out of her suit jacket and hung it over Melanie's shoulders.

"No, you'll get cold," Melanie protested.

Shannon waved her off. "You're giving me an excuse to get out of this constricting thing. How about we all head to my house for coffee?"

"Sounds good to me," Joyce said.

"Me too," Kate said, hugging the Beagle pup close. "I'll drop this little guy off at my place on the way."

As they walked to their vehicles, they passed many curious onlookers whose accusatory whispers could be heard as they slipped through the crowd. When they reached the other side of the road, Shannon helped Melanie into Joyce's white minivan and inhaled the lingering scent of fresh baked goods. As owner of Pink Sprinkles Bakery, Joyce had provided a beautiful cake topped with an iced drawing of the new coffee shop, Espresso Yourself, for the ceremony. A cake that had gone completely untouched.

Kate took a long, appreciative sniff as she passed by the open door. "Oh, man. Your car always smells so much better than mine, Joyce."

"Hey, if my van doesn't smell better than a dog groomer's car, I should be thrown out of the bakery business," Joyce joked, as she cranked the engine.

The others chuckled—even Melanie—and the overall mood lifted a little.

"I'll see you all back at the house." Shannon waited until the other ladies' vehicles pulled away from the curb, then she made her way around the back of her shop to the narrow alley where she'd parked her truck. The bright blue pickup had once belonged to her grandfather, James Paisley. Despite the 1955 Ford's mechanical issues, she smiled every time she climbed inside and sat on the bench seat.

She jerked the groaning door closed and cranked the engine. The motor moaned and heaved, coughing like an asthmatic, then sputtered to life. She soon chugged out of the picturesque downtown square, leaving the dreadful scene behind.

As she drove into the country, a slight drizzle wetted

her windshield. It wasn't enough to turn on the wipers, just enough to dampen everything around her. Having recently relocated from Scotland, Shannon thought she'd have a hard time adjusting to Oregon weather. Not so. She felt right at home with the coast's cool temperatures and frequent rainy days.

She turned onto a long driveway, winding up the lane to the 1930s Mediterranean-style mansion she'd recently inherited from her grandmother, Victoria Paisley. Shannon loved everything about the property, from the stucco facade painted in warm putty, with its round turrets and terra-cotta tiled roof, to the lush grounds with a wondrous assortment of vibrant perennials. Though more formal than Shannon was used to, the place already felt like home.

She hurried up the curved stone stairs, unlocked the door, and stepped aside to let her friends enter the large foyer.

Kate stopped inside the door and turned in circles, as if seeing the place for the first time. "I'd totally think I had died and gone to heaven if I inherited property like this," she said, her voice a mixture of awe and jealousy. "Of course, there's no one in my family who owns a place this amazing, so that will never happen."

"Hey," Shannon said, "I never even knew my Grandmother Paisley existed until she left Paisley Manor to me. Who knows, Kate? You may have a long-lost relative somewhere out there just like her."

"No such luck." Kate grinned. "All of my grandparents are present and accounted for."

Shannon led the way into the kitchen. She settled Melanie on a wrought iron stool at the large granite island, then kicked off her shoes and sighed. "Thank goodness I don't have to wear pumps every day."

"I'm surprised you got so dressed up," Kate said, as she slipped her jacket off to reveal one of her many animal-themed shirts. "No one around here does that much, except maybe for church or a funeral."

Melanie sucked in a breath.

"Oh, Mel." Kate circled the island and put an arm around her friend. "I'm so sorry. I wasn't thinking."

"It's OK. Really, it is," Melanie assured her.

"What we all need is sugar, and lots of it," Shannon announced. She strode to the butler's pantry where she'd stashed the evidence of recent long, lonely nights filled with baking. She pulled out three containers of different kinds of cookies and set them on the center island. Then she crossed over to the professional-grade refrigerator and removed a candy apple pie and Melanie's favorite dessert, a chocolate chip cheesecake.

When she turned, she caught four sets of curious eyes watching her.

"What?" She laughed as she set the pie and cheesecake on the island. "I like to bake. So shoot me."

Melanie winced again, and Shannon flashed an apologetic smile for the grim remark.

"C'mon, Shannon, 'fess up." Joyce perched on a stool next to Kate and watched Shannon dash across the kitchen to the coffee pot with motherly concern. "You only bake because you miss your twins."

"Don't look so worried, Joyce. I'm fine," said Shannon as she poured freshly roasted Guatemalan coffee beans into the pot. The built in grinder whirred as it ground the beans Betty had given to Shannon not long after she'd arrived from Scotland in an attempt to convert her to a coffee drinker—a near-requirement for living in Oregon.

"Right." Joyce pulled silverware from the drawer next to her. "You're just as fine as Betty and I were when our kids first left home."

"It does get better, you know." Betty grabbed a stack of small plates from the cupboard. "But it takes some of us longer to recover than others."

"You're referring to me, I suppose," Shannon said.

"Actually, I meant Joyce." Betty winked at Joyce. "She cried like a baby for two months."

Joyce playfully punched Betty's arm. "I'll have you know there are days when I still can't believe they're grown and gone. I go into one of their bedrooms for something, and it hits me all over again how empty it feels without them in the house. And then, yes, I cry like a baby!"

Shannon laughed with her new friends as she plated the first piece of rich cheesecake and handed it to Melanie. "I don't know what I'd do without all of you to help me get through this."

"You'll pack on fifty pounds if you keep baking like this and eating it all yourself," Kate finally chimed in.

Shannon watched her eye the cheesecake with longing and felt a twinge of guilt for tempting her friend with sweets. It was no secret Kate struggled mightily to keep her weight in check.

"At least you have Deborah to help you eat all the goodies you bake," Betty said, settling onto a stool.

"Actually, after all the recent excitement of finding my grandmother's hidden necklace, she took off this morning on a little getaway to visit a friend," Shannon said, thinking about how her housekeeper must be enjoying her peaceful drive up the coast after the dangerous events of the previous month. "She'll be gone for a week or so."

"Won't it be odd living in this big old house by yourself?" Melanie stuck her fork into the cheesecake, but she didn't cut a bite.

"It will certainly be different." Shannon cleaned off the knife, the gooey cheesecake clinging to it the way she wanted to cling to her children. "But it will give me a chance to explore all the nooks and crannies in private."

"Oh, I almost forgot," Betty said. "Your mother told me to tell you she was sorry she had to leave during the frenzy today. One of her employees called in sick, and she had to hurry back to Portland to fill in for him. She said she'd give you a call later."

With all of Shannon's worries about Melanie, she hadn't even noticed that her mother had disappeared—probably because she still hadn't gotten used to the idea of her reappearance in her life.

When Shannon was just 4, her mother had disappeared without a trace. Shannon grew up never knowing what happened to her, or if she was even alive. But thanks to her grandmother's will, which is what brought Shannon to Apple Grove, she was reunited with her mother once again, and she'd learned of the dire circumstances that caused her mother to abandon her and her father all those years ago. But the truth was she still hadn't completely made peace with it in her heart.

Betty held out her plate toward Shannon. "As much as I love your cheesecake, I think I need a big piece of that pie."

As the rich aroma of coffee filled the kitchen, Shannon sliced through the many layers of the award-winning pie she'd seen on a television show. She slipped the server under a graham cracker crust layered with nuts. Caramel topping oozed out the side as she lifted a large piece overflowing with Granny Smith apples sautéed in butter, brown sugar and cinnamon, and topped with a cream cheese filling, then settled it onto a plate.

"Who else wants pie?" she asked as she slid the plate across the island to Betty.

"Are you kidding?" Kate laughed. "I've gained five pounds just being in the same room as that pie. I'm settling for a cup of coffee and one cookie."

"Your willpower is astounding, kiddo," Joyce said, eyeing the pie. "I wish I could say no, but it looks too good to pass up."

The phone rang from the other side of the kitchen.

"I'll leave you to dish it up yourself." Shannon handed the server to Joyce then, crossed the room to retrieve the wireless handset, licking her sticky fingers as she went.

"Hello," she answered, and leaned against the counter, keeping a close eye on Melanie. Despite the group's obvious effort to keep the mood light and off the subject of Edward's death, she hadn't eaten a single bite of her cheesecake.

"Grayson here," the deep voice boomed through the phone, and Shannon felt a sense of foreboding settle in her heart.

"Grayson," she said loudly, so the others wouldn't inadvertently say something the chief might overhear. Their conversations came to an abrupt stop.

"Is Melanie still with you?" he asked.

"Yes."

"We have some preliminary information about Ed's death, and I'd like to stop by to discuss it with her."

"What kind of information?"

"You must believe I'm some country bumpkin of a cop if you think I'd share that information with you now and give Melanie time to come up with a story before I get there."

"I wasn't thinking that at all. Let me ask Melanie if she feels like talking to you." Shannon cupped her hand over the phone. "Grayson has some preliminary information about Ed's death, and he wants to stop by to talk to you about it."

Melanie's fork clattered to the plate. "You mean he wants to ask me where I was at the time when he died, right? To see if I have an alibi?"

"That would be my guess," Shannon said, not liking the way Melanie had paled again.

Melanie clasped her hands together, squeezing the blood from her fingers. "It's not like he'll go away, so I might as well get the conversation over with."

Shannon nodded, then returned her attention to the phone. "You may stop by for a few minutes."

"I'm on my way," he said a little too eagerly for Shannon's liking.

Shannon hung up and studied Melanie. She'd been through so much in the last year with her struggle to over-come breast cancer. She didn't deserve another hardship so soon, and she especially didn't deserve the turmoil Edward's murder would bring into her life.

As Shannon rejoined her new friends, she prayed that Melanie would have an alibi for the time when Edward had met his demise. Otherwise, Shannon feared her dear friend's life was about to take a very dark turn.

3

Shannon settled the coffee tray on a mahogany table in the drawing room, near a large mural of ocean waves breaking on the beach below dark tumultuous skies. The mural, painted by her mother many years before, reflected the mood in the house. The Purls had moved to this very formal room in anticipation of Grayson's visit. The space, filled with traditional furnishings, was perfect for reminding Melanie not to relax or let her guard down for even a second with the chief.

Shannon carried her steaming cup across the room, keeping a careful eye on Melanie. Even with the Purls attempts to cheer her up, she looked lost and defeated sitting in the large, overstuffed chair. It was clear she was holding on by the narrowest of threads.

Shannon sat in the wingback chair next to her and sipped her coffee.

"I really appreciate all of you offering to go with me to talk to Greg," Melanie twisted the hem of her blue-and-white striped shirt between her fingers, "but I'm worried that if we all show up on his doorstep, we'll overwhelm him."

"But you can't go alone." Betty appraised Melanie with a motherly look. "At least let one of us come along."

Melanie shook her head. "I know you only took the morning off for the dedication ceremony and you all have jobs to go back to. I couldn't take you from your work this afternoon too."

"Grayson has the shop cordoned off, so I can't open today anyway," Shannon said. "I have nothing to do and I'm free to go."

Melanie shot her a thankful look. "Are you sure?"

"Positive."

"Well," Melanie said, "I'd like to leave as soon as the chief is finished with me, is that OK with you?"

"Of course." Shannon didn't think the chief would be truly finished with Melanie until he'd solved Edward's murder, but she thought it wise to keep her suspicion to herself.

"Can I ask another favor, Shannon?" Melanie asked, as she slid forward on her chair.

"Anything."

"It's clear to me that Grayson thinks I killed Ed. If I don't have an alibi for his time of death, do you think you could look into the murder for me?"

Shannon blinked. "*Me?*"

"Yeah. I know you watch all of those crime shows, so you know how they always suspect the spouse. Even though Ed and I weren't still married, I'm afraid that if I don't have an alibi, the chief won't bother trying to find the real killer."

"She may be right, Shannon," Kate said, sounding so sure of herself, though she, like the others, had zero experience with a murder investigation. "And you did such a good job of figuring out the mystery your grandmother left behind, I'm sure you could figure this out too."

"Will you do it?" Melanie pressed. "Please?"

Shannon wasn't sure how much help she could be, but

Melanie's look of desperation had her nodding. "Of course, I will."

The doorbell rang, and Melanie jumped.

"That must be Grayson, I'll let him in. Try and relax." Shannon gave Melanie's shoulder a reassuring pat then hurried into the foyer. She opened the door, but blocked Grayson's entrance with her body. "Before you get started, I want you to know Melanie is extremely distraught. It would be helpful if you were sympathetic to that."

Grayson looked at Shannon for a long moment, his expression unreadable. "I don't like having to question her, but the tone of our conversation is solely up to her. If she cooperates with me, things will go easier for her."

She narrowed her eyes at him, giving him an unspoken warning, before moving to allow him to step inside. She led him down the hall, his footfalls clumping loudly on the tile floor. When they entered the drawing room, she could feel the tension hanging in the air.

"Please have a seat," she offered as she perched on the rolled arm of Melanie's chair.

Grayson didn't sit. He stood looking down on them. "I understand that all of you want to support Melanie, but this conversation is confidential, so I'm afraid I'll have to ask you to leave."

Melanie clutched at Shannon's leg as if she feared being alone with him.

Shannon didn't want to start the meeting in an antagonistic way, but she also didn't want to leave Melanie alone. "This has been so hard on Melanie," Shannon said. "If we can't sit in with her as witnesses, I'm afraid she'll have to contact a lawyer before answering your questions."

"Now don't go getting all uppity, Shannon." He fisted his hands. "Melanie doesn't need a lawyer or a witness. I'm simply going to discuss some things with her that I don't want released to the public yet."

"We promise we won't tell anyone what you say," Joyce jumped in.

He started to roll his eyes, but must have thought better of it and stopped. "I appreciate the offer, but the fewer people who know about this, the better."

As she felt Melanie's nails dig deeper into her leg, Shannon knew she had to try harder to remain by her friend's side. "You've asked for my expertise in the case, and that means I'll already have access to confidential information," she said. "So I might as well stay. What's one more piece of information that I have to keep quiet?"

Grayson seemed to weigh Shannon's words. She folded her hands on her lap and waited patiently, listening to the *tick, tick, tick* of the large grandfather clock against the wall.

Finally, Grayson gave a reluctant nod. "Shannon can stay, but the rest of you will have to go."

Immediately, Shannon felt Melanie's fingers loosen their death grip on her leg. "I'll call everyone later and update you on anything I'm allowed to tell you," she said.

The other women rose slowly. Each of them hugged Melanie, and Shannon watched Grayson as they did so. She expected him to be upset with the delay, but it didn't seem to bother him. Instead, his expression filled with compassion as he studied Melanie. Shannon felt bad for thinking he was out to get her friend. Perhaps he really was a good guy stuck doing a thankless job. She'd heard around town that he was usually fair and impartial, and everyone seemed to like him.

He'll do the right thing here, won't he?

"The way the girls looked at me, you'd think I was going before a firing squad." Melanie said, attempting to laugh, but it came out flat and dull.

Shannon settled into a chair near Melanie and listened as the Purls retrieved their belongings from the foyer.

Grayson grabbed a straight-backed chair and slid it close to Melanie. "As I told you earlier, Melanie, I am very sorry for your loss. Please give your son my condolences."

"I will. Thank you," Melanie whispered, tears forming in her eyes.

"If I didn't have to bother you right now, I wouldn't," he said. "But the first 48 hours after a homicide are very important in an investigation. The sooner I can rule people out as suspects, the sooner I can find the killer."

"I understand."

He cleared his throat, and in a flash, he transitioned from a concerned neighbor to a hard-as-nails cop. "Let's start by you telling me where you were between 7 p.m. and 9 p.m. yesterday."

His tone set off alarm bells in Shannon's head.

"I was on my nightly walk," Melanie said without hesitation.

"For two hours?" Grayson's eyes narrowed with suspicion.

She nodded. "Whenever the weather allows, I take a long walk, then sit on the beach and watch the sunset as I cool down."

"And where did this walk take place?"

"Old Beach Trail."

Grayson leaned closer. "Anyone go with you?"

"No."

Shannon saw the gleam in Grayson's eye as he quickly jotted a note on his pad.

"Did you see or talk to anyone else during your walk?" he asked.

"No. The point of walking on that stretch of beach is that it's quiet, and I have solitude. It's a dead-end street with easy access to the beach, so there's never any traffic, and I can clear my—" Melanie stopped abruptly. "Wait— that was when Edward was killed, isn't it?"

Grayson didn't respond.

"I can't believe this is happening. Ed was killed between 7 p.m. and 9 p.m., and I have no alibi during that time." Melanie sat up straight in her chair, showing signs of the strong woman Shannon had recently come to know. "I know what you're thinking, but I *didn't* kill Ed."

"But there was no love lost between you—was there?"

Melanie crossed her arms. "There was nothing between us at all. He was out of my life for good. And, as I've said repeatedly, I didn't kill him. No matter what he did to me, he's still my son's father. Between my cancer and my divorce, Greg's been through enough. I'd never contemplate causing him additional suffering by killing his father. I'd never contemplate killing *anyone* for *any* reason, for that matter."

"Maybe not intentionally." Grayson eyed her like a hungry lion. "But people do things in the heat of passion that they never thought possible."

Shannon cleared her throat to draw his attention away from her friend for a moment. "If the murder *was* committed in the heat of passion as you said, then you have to admit the odds that Melanie would have a knitting needle with her at that precise moment are pretty slim."

"That's right," Melanie added. "Anyway, everyone knows it's not safe to knit and argue at the same time." She ended with a forced laugh, but her attempt at humor was lost on Grayson. He continued to stare at her, uncertain how to respond.

Shannon had no inclination to laugh either. This was serious. Very serious. Melanie didn't have an alibi. A coincidence? Shannon didn't think so. If the person who killed Edward knew Melanie's daily routine, he could have chosen a certain time of day to set her up for the murder.

"Did you drive to Old Beach Trail?" Grayson asked, his tone somber.

"Yes."

"So your knitting supplies would've been in your car, right?"

"No. I don't ever leave them in my car after work. I always knit while I watch *Wheel of Fortune*, and that's what I did last night."

"You're sure?" he asked.

She nodded vigorously. "Positive. I was working on a difficult pattern I'd been having trouble with, and I wanted to try one more time to get it right before having to ask the group for help. I ate a frozen meal for supper and then went straight to work on it." Melanie turned to Shannon. "You'll be happy to hear I worked it out."

"That's great." Shannon said, amazed Melanie could even *think* about a sweater she was knitting at the moment.

"Unfortunately, you were alone the entire time," Grayson

said, reclaiming their attention. "And that means I can't rule you out as a suspect."

"Doesn't a suspect need a motive for murder?" Melanie challenged. "I had no reason to kill Ed."

Grayson scoffed. "That's not what I've heard."

"I don't know what people are saying, but sure, I *was* upset with him when he bailed on me—a time when I needed him the most," Melanie said. "But that's in the past, and I'm over it. I know I'm better off without him."

"And," Shannon added, "even when she was angry at him, she didn't want to kill him."

Melanie nodded. "That's right. I'll admit that I wished he would suffer. Not because of what he did to me, but for the pain it caused our son. That's—"

Shannon held up her hand, warning Melanie hush.

"What?" Melanie asked. "It's the truth. Although I may have wished for it, I'd never do anything to cause it. Hurting Ed would've only hurt Greg more."

Grayson studied her for a long moment. "I have to admit your story sounds good, but without proof of your whereabouts at the time of death, I'm afraid you'll remain on our suspect list."

"Who else is on that list?" Shannon interjected. If she was going to be any good as a detective she knew she needed to start asking some key questions.

"It's still early in the investigation, and we haven't identified anyone else." Grayson focused on Melanie. "Who do you think would want to kill him?"

"I can't think of anyone in our past life together who would want him dead. And I don't know a thing about his current life in Portland, so I can't begin to speculate about that."

"When's the last time you saw him?" Grayson asked.

"He was at a housewarming party that my son, Greg, threw in Portland last year."

"Was he there alone?"

"No," Melanie said. "He came with a date—I think her name was Angie. I don't remember her last name, but Greg might know it."

"I'll need your son's contact information so I can call him." Grayson handed Melanie his notebook and pen. "Can you jot down his number and address for me?"

She started to write, then paused and held the pen above the paper. "Would you mind not calling Greg until I have a chance to tell him what happened to Ed?"

"Depends. When do you plan to do that?"

"We're heading to Portland right after you finish with us," Shannon interjected, half expecting him to argue with her about Melanie leaving town.

"That will be fine," Grayson said. "But I'd appreciate it if you'd give me a call as soon as you talk to him."

"OK." Melanie scribbled a phone number on the page. Then she handed the notebook back to Grayson.

Tucking it into his pocket, he stood up to leave. "One more thing. Have you spoken to Ed since the party?"

"No. I didn't even speak to him *at* the party."

"You're sure?"

Melanie paused, chewing her lip. "Positive."

"So when we request your phone records, we won't find any calls made to or received from Ed?" Grayson fixed Melanie with a hard look.

"My phone records?" Melanie repeated, then paused as if considering the question. "Um ... no, of course not."

"OK, then," he said, eyeing her suspiciously. "That's all for now. If you plan on taking any trips other than the one to Portland, I'd appreciate it if you'd let me know in advance."

Melanie looked at him accusingly. "You honestly consider me a suspect, don't you?"

"I'm sorry, Melanie, but since you don't have an alibi, I have no other choice." He tipped his head in the direction of the hall. "I'll see myself out."

"I'm so sorry, sweetie," Shannon said after he left. "I hate that he's putting you through this."

Melanie tucked her hands under her knees and nervously wiggled her legs. "I didn't kill Ed. You believe me, don't you?"

"Of course I do, and so does everyone who knows you." Shannon offered Melanie a reassuring smile.

"This is a nightmare." Melanie stood and began to pace in front of the large window that overlooked the expansive front lawn. "It's like those cases you see on television where the cop focuses on only one person, the *wrong* person, while the real killer goes free."

"Hey, let's not panic. From everything I've heard about Grayson, he's good at his job. Plus, he has no hard evidence against you."

Melanie came to an abrupt stop. "But that's not my biggest problem, is it? The problem seems to be that there's nothing to prove I *didn't* do it either. I have no alibi." She ran her fingers through her hair and turned to face the window. "Too bad it had to happen while I was on the beach. What are the odds of that—like a million to one?"

"Not if the time of the murder was *planned* to coincide with your walk," Shannon said.

Melanie spun around to face her. "What do you mean?"

"I suspect someone is trying to frame you for this murder, and they knew exactly when you'd be alone—leaving you without an alibi."

"Frame *me*? That seems a little far-fetched."

Shannon sat forward on her chair. "Think about it. Edward's death occurred at a time of day when you're known to be alone. He was killed with a knitting needle that's similar to one you might own, and I didn't want to tell you this, but I'm pretty sure the yarn used to bind his hands is the same yarn you're using for the sweater you're knitting for Greg's 30th birthday."

Melanie gasped and her face paled. "But why would someone do this? And *who*?"

"It could be anyone who wanted Edward dead and knew that your bitter breakup would make you the perfect patsy."

"That's great," Melanie said sarcastically, throwing her hands up into the air. "That does nothing to narrow the list of suspects. Everyone in town knew about our bitter divorce."

"True, but not everyone in town wanted to kill Ed, did they?"

Melanie laughed, but there was no mirth in her voice. "No. People liked him. Even *I* liked him, until he deserted me during my darkest hour."

"That's good then, isn't it? Our suspect pool will be small, and it will be easier to figure out who wanted him dead."

Melanie sighed. "You make it sound so easy, but I

wouldn't even know where to start."

Shannon didn't know either, but after the visit from Grayson, she had a hunch. "Since Greg is the only one who's been in touch with Edward lately, I think it would be beneficial to talk to him about these things. He may know something."

Melanie circled her arms around her middle, as if protecting herself from the tragedy.

Shannon put a comforting arm around her friend's shoulders. "I understand you don't want to bring Greg into this. I know what it's like for a son to lose his father, and I'd never suggest it if I didn't think it was the best idea right now."

Melanie exhaled a long breath and squared her shoulders. "OK. I know I can't put this off, better to get it over with."

Shannon hugged Melanie close. "We'll get to the bottom of this, I promise."

Although Shannon made every effort to project confidence, the bravado was all a show. A heavy ball of dread had lodged in the pit of her stomach the moment she'd learned Melanie had no alibi. It occurred to her that if Edward's killer was smart enough to frame Melanie for the crime, he was likely already two steps ahead of them.

Catching him wasn't going to be nearly as easy as she'd made it sound.

4

Standing in Greg's small kitchen, Shannon grabbed the coffee pot he had put on to brew when they'd first arrived. She filled three large stoneware mugs with the aromatic java and inhaled deeply as the full-bodied, nutty scent rose up to greet her. Although nothing would ever replace tea in her heart, she was beginning to like coffee more and more, especially when it was freshly ground.

She loaded the tray with milk and sugar, then set off for the living room. In the hallway, she paused to listen.

"Stop worrying, Mom," Greg said, his voice gentle. "I'll be fine."

"I wish you didn't have to go through this." Melanie's tone carried a heavy dose of anguish.

Shannon's heart constricted as she recalled the nightmare of having to break the same horrible news to Alec and Lara about the death of their father. She wished there was something she could do to make it easier for Melanie and ease her pain.

"You haven't told me. Do the police know who did this?" Greg asked.

"No, but I don't think we can count on them to find the killer. Fortunately, Shannon has agreed to help me investigate."

There was a long pause in the conversation. Shannon imagined Greg must be looking at his mother like she was nuts. She herself still doubted that she could solve the murder, so Greg had every right to be skeptical.

"No offense to your friend, Mom, but what kind of training does she have that qualifies her to find a killer?"

"She may not have actual hands-on experience tracking down a killer, but she recently worked through a very complicated mystery surrounding her late grandmother. I'm certain she can do the same thing for me."

"Uh-huh," Greg said. "Even so, I think you all should leave this to the police to investigate."

Shannon thought he might change his tune if he knew Melanie was the prime suspect, but Melanie had insisted they not tell him.

"Trust me, Son, I know what I'm doing, and so does Shannon."

Shannon's confidence was buoyed by the conviction in Melanie's voice. *I will not let her down.* She entered the room and set the tray on an oversize ottoman that doubled as a coffee table. She wanted to launch right into questioning Greg, but thought it would be better for Melanie or Greg to initiate the conversation, so she handed a mug to each of them without saying a word. Melanie accepted hers with a smile of thanks, but Greg shook his head. Shannon cradled the warm mug in her hands and lowered herself into a chair.

"So, Greg." Melanie paused and shared a knowing look with Shannon. "Do you have any thoughts on who might want to do something like this to your dad?"

He shook his head, his face tilting toward the ceiling as if he might find the answer there. "I don't know ... I mean, *murder*? What kind of person commits murder?"

Shannon appraised him over the rim of her mug. He had his mother's sturdy build, but he was several inches taller. He looked at Shannon, and his emerald eyes implored her to respond to his question.

"I think a person would have to be pretty desperate to commit murder," Shannon said. "We're probably looking for someone whose back was against the wall and couldn't think of another way out."

"I can't think of anyone like that," he answered, sounding lost.

"If it helps narrow things down, it's most likely someone who lives in Apple Grove," Shannon said. "Or at the very least someone who has a tie to the town."

"Why would you say that?" Greg asked.

Shannon shrugged. "Because Edward's body was dumped in Apple Grove—not his home town of Portland."

Greg winced, and Shannon instantly regretted speaking so plainly.

"She's right, Greg." Melanie set down her mug and scooted closer to her son. "I've tried to come up with someone in Apple Grove who'd want to kill him, but I can't. Everyone there liked him. I was wondering if it could be someone in his current life, but still someone who knows about Apple Grove."

Greg shook his head. "But who? Dad lives here. His life is in Portland now. Other than you meeting his girlfriend, Angie, at my party, there's no connection to Apple Grove that I know of."

"What about Angie, then?" Shannon asked Greg. "Were things good between them? And, by chance, do you know her last name?"

"Carson. Her last name is Carson. I don't know much about her relationship with Dad. He never talked about her, but they seemed happy." Greg took Melanie's hands between his, completely engulfing them. "I hate to say this, but I kind of like Angie. She is—was—kind to Dad and supportive. I can't imagine Angie as a killer."

A tense silence filled the room, and Shannon guessed Melanie was uncomfortable with the topic. Not that Shannon blamed her. If she were Melanie, she'd have cringed when Greg admitted to liking the new girlfriend.

"Maybe it had to do with his job," Shannon suggested, attempting to change the topic.

"Perhaps." Greg released Melanie's hands and sat back. "But I don't know how taking people on sightseeing tours could lead to murder."

"Still, it might be a good place to start," Shannon said. "Can you tell us the name of the company he worked for?"

Greg shook his head. "Sorry. I suppose I should know it, but he rarely talked about his work."

Melanie held up a hand. "Before you ask, Shannon, I don't know either."

Greg rubbed his chin, thinking. "He should have paycheck stubs or some sort of job information at his apartment," he said. "I have a key, I could go look."

Melanie shook her head. "I couldn't ask you to go over there so soon after losing him."

"I'll do it if it will help find his killer."

"We could come with you," Melanie suggested, glancing at Shannon.

Shannon nodded her agreement.

"Are you sure?" he asked.

"Absolutely."

Greg cast a wary look at his mother. "I'll need to find Angie's phone number and give her a quick call while we're there to let her know what's happened. I hope that won't upset you."

Melanie's eyes glistened with tears as she took her son's hand. "You're a good person, thinking of others when you have to be hurting. I'm so proud of the man you've become."

Greg hugged his mom, and as Melanie looked up, Shannon could see in her eyes what she wasn't saying. More than anything, she was glad he was more responsible than his father had been.

"We should get going," Greg said, pulling away from Melanie. "I'll turn off the coffee pot and meet you outside."

Shannon and Melanie stepped wordlessly into the light rain spitting from the darkened sky. The chilly drizzle further dampened an already wet mood, but Shannon put on a false smile and turned to Melanie. "Greg appears to be handling the news well."

"He's such a strong person." The pride Melanie felt in her son colored her words. "God has truly blessed me with Greg."

"Indeed. I feel the same way about my twins."

"I look forward to meeting them," Melanie said. "I'll bet you can hardly wait until the semester at St. Andrew's ends and they move here."

Shannon sighed. "It will be wonderful to have them close to me again." She often daydreamed about the day when they would finally finish their first year at university in Scotland and hop on a plane to Oregon. Each time the vision came to mind, her heart warmed.

But now was not the time to be daydreaming about her children. It was time to help Melanie.

*   *   *

When the female robo-voice on the GPS announced their final turn, Melanie slowed her SUV, then pulled into a large parking lot connected to a high-rise apartment complex on the outskirts of downtown Portland. Greg got out first and came around the car to open both Shannon and Melanie's doors.

"The main entrance is over there." He pointed across the lot. "If we hurry, we won't get too wet."

Melanie lifted her hood, and Shannon held her hands over her hair. Why, she didn't know. Her curly mop frizzed at even a hint of moisture, so the damage was already done.

Greg led them to a building where light spilled out from floor-to-ceiling windows, making the steel structure feel somewhat welcoming. He swiped a magnetic key card through the card reader next to the entrance, and the door lock clunked. He held the door open and they all slipped into the sleek, modern lobby. Black leather chairs with chrome legs and shiny glass coffee tables were arranged in intimate seating areas. Purple area rugs, boasting swirls of red and turquoise, covered the floor.

Melanie turned in a full circle, taking it all in. "Not the kind of place I ever expected Ed to live."

"He said he wanted to live the single life he never experienced," Greg said as he punched the elevator button.

Shannon shared an irritated look with Melanie. *If Edward had wanted a bachelor's lifestyle, he never should have married Melanie and had a child.*

Once they arrived on the tenth floor, Greg led them down a hallway lit with chrome wall fixtures and carpeted in a bold, purple color that matched the lobby rugs. He stopped outside the last apartment and slipped a key in the lock. Before the key clicked into place, the door slid open.

Shannon felt a chill run up her spine.

"Someone's here," Greg observed, looking puzzled.

"Maybe it's Angie," Melanie said.

"As far as I know, I'm the only other person with a key." Greg continued to stare at the opened door as if he expected someone to race out.

"We should call the police." Melanie reached for his arm and pulled him back.

"No," Shannon said quickly. "If we call the police, we'll never get to look inside."

"But someone could be in there," Melanie protested.

Shannon stepped over the threshold before Greg or Melanie could stop her. "Hello?" she called out.

"Stop, Shannon." Greg eased in front of her and gave her an exasperated look so reminiscent of Melanie's expressions that, despite Shannon's unease over finding the apartment open, she had to grin a little.

"You two wait here," he said. "I'll check it out."

"He's a chip off the old block," Shannon said.

"What?" Melanie's worried gaze followed her son as he flipped on a light and walked farther inside.

"He looks exactly like you do when he gets perturbed."

"If he gets into any trouble in there, you're going to see much more than a perturbed look from me." She wrinkled her nose at Shannon, and her glasses wobbled.

Shannon smiled at her friend. It felt so good to smile. An honest-to-goodness smile. The day had been filled with far too much sadness and worry.

Greg returned to the door. "Someone's been here, all right—the place is trashed. But whoever it was is gone now."

Eager to see what he meant by "trashed," Shannon pushed past him and through a small foyer leading into a compact family room. As she caught sight of the space, she stopped and stared. Greg was right. Someone had completely trashed the apartment.

The typical bachelor living room boasted black leather furniture, a monster-size television, and speakers of equal size. The TV and speakers still sat upright in their places, but the cushions had all been shredded and discarded on the floor. Drawers had been pulled from a desk built into the bookshelves and their contents dumped out, and DVDs littered the beige carpeting.

It was obvious to Shannon that it was not a typical burglary. Someone had been looking for something specific, otherwise the TV and stereo equipment would be missing.

"Who would do this?" Melanie asked from behind.

"I don't know, but we have to call the police," Greg insisted.

"Just give me a few minutes to look around first," Shannon said as she eased into the room, stepping gingerly over cushions and around the contents from the shelves. "I don't think this break-in is a coincidence."

"You think the killer was here?" Greg asked.

Shannon nodded and thought about where to start as her gaze landed on Ed's computer. Investigators on her favorite crime shows always looked at computers for emails and Internet history. *As good a place to start as any.*

Using the sleeve of her shirt so she didn't leave any prints, Shannon jiggled the mouse. The screen woke up, and she had to smile when she saw that Ed had left his email program open, eliminating the need for a password. She selected all of the emails in his Inbox and Sent folders, plus his Address Book, then sent the files to the printer.

"I don't feel right about being here," Melanie whispered from her position in the doorway.

"It's OK, Mom. I have a key and Dad would want me to let you in so we can figure this out." Greg joined Shannon in the living room and started sorting through paperwork scattered on the floor.

"You should stay right where you are, Mel, and don't touch a thing." Shannon gave her friend a warning look. "We don't want you to leave any fingerprints and give the police another reason to suspect you."

Greg's head popped up, his face a roadmap of tension. "They suspect you?"

"They always suspect the spouse or ex," Shannon answered quickly to cover up her gaffe. She held her breath, hoping he wouldn't ask any additional questions. When he switched his focus back to the files, Shannon exhaled and turned back to the computer. She selected Edward's Internet browser history and bookmarks, and started them printing as well.

"How do you know what's important on there?" Melanie called out from the doorway.

"I don't," Shannon said. "I'm going for the same things I see them look for on television cop shows." She heard Greg mutter something under his breath and decided she didn't care to know what he'd said.

"Good thing for me you watch all those dreadful programs," Melanie said.

Shannon glanced over at her friend, whose television viewing trended toward gardening and history. "I never thought I'd hear you say that."

"I think I've found his will." Greg flipped through the pages in a black folder.

"I can't imagine he had anything of real value that would require a will," Melanie remarked.

"Everyone should have a will, Mom." Greg ran his fingers down a page, then turned it. "And he must've had *something* of value. This will was recently drawn up by a top legal firm, and there'd be no point in paying those kinds of attorney's fees if he didn't need to."

Melanie pursed her lips. "Then either he hid assets when we got divorced, or he's come into some money lately."

Shannon looked up in time to catch the suspicion in Melanie's eyes before she veiled it, likely for Greg's sake.

"Can you take care of checking into his assets, Greg?" Shannon asked. "His bank account might give us a lead."

"Yeah, I can do that." He looked at his mother. "I'll let you know what I find out."

As the printer spit out pages, Shannon searched the computer for any information about Edward's employer, but she came up empty. She rose from her chair and approached Greg. "If you find any credit card statements, phone bills, receipts, or information about your dad's employer, would you make copies for me?"

"Sure," he answered without looking up from the document was examining.

"I'm going to take a quick peek into the other rooms," said Shannon, meeting Melanie's gaze. "Before you ask, the receipts and statements can help us figure out where he's been the last month or so, and the phone bills might give us more info about his job and anyone who might have it in for him."

"This new PI role suits you well." Melanie's lips curved in a smile.

Shannon grinned back at her and then disappeared down the hallway leading to Edward's bedroom. She felt odd going into his most personal space, but she had to do it for Melanie. The small room had been tossed in the same manner—mattress tipped over, drawers dumped out—but all Shannon could see were clothes strewn about.

In the bathroom, the small linen closet stood empty, and bottles were smashed on the floor. She chose not to step inside, as she'd then track the contents throughout the apartment and confuse the police. By the time she'd searched a hall closet and returned to the main living space, Greg had moved next to the printer.

"I'm almost done here," he said, holding a stack of papers.

"Did you find Angie's phone number?" Shannon asked.

"Yeah. I'll call her after I call the police."

Shannon faced Melanie. "We shouldn't be here when the police arrive."

"She's right, Mom." Greg tapped the pages into a neat

pile. "You all should go. I'll call a friend to come and pick me up."

Melanie shook her head. "I can't do that."

"I'll be fine. I can handle this." He grabbed the last of the pages from the printer and walked toward them.

As he did, Shannon couldn't help but notice Melanie's overprotective nature toward her son. Shannon recognized the trait; she felt the same way about Alec and Lara. But right now, Melanie really needed to think of herself first.

"He's right," Shannon said, taking the copies from Greg. "He's more than capable of handling this."

"Go," Greg urged.

"You're sure?" asked Melanie.

"Positive." He hugged Melanie, then turned her around by the shoulders and gave her a gentle push toward the door. "I'll call you in the morning."

"How about tonight when you get home?" Melanie stopped walking and peered up at him. "With everything that's happened, I want to make sure you get home OK. Otherwise, I won't get a wink of sleep."

"I'm not a kid anymore, Mom. I'm almost 30, remember?" He pulled back his shoulders, looking exactly like a taller, male version of Melanie when she'd stood up to Grayson. After a brief stare down with Melanie, he let out an exasperated sigh. "OK, fine. If it will help you sleep, I'll call you when I get home. But don't think this means I'm going back to the old days, when I checked in repeatedly just to ease your overactive imagination."

"Don't worry, Son. I know you're all grown up and have your own life."

Melanie didn't seem hurt by his comment. If her own son had said the same thing to her, Shannon wasn't sure she would've taken it in stride so well.

"Would you mind driving again?" Melanie asked as they exited the building.

"No problem." Glad to get out of the cold, Shannon unlocked the door and climbed behind the wheel.

Once on the road, Melanie rested her head on the window, seemingly lost in her thoughts.

They climbed out of the city, leaving behind twinkling lights and the many bridges spanning the Willamette River. Suburban shopping centers and houses soon disappeared, replaced by tall pine trees grouped forest-close. The road narrowed and wound through the Coast Range, climbing higher and higher, and making her ears pop.

"I've been thinking," Melanie said, finally breaking her silence as they made the downward descent from the mountains. "I know the chief has put his focus on me because he thinks I have the best motive to kill Ed, but what if this isn't about me at all? What if it's about you?"

"*Me?*" Shannon felt her jaw drop. "I didn't even *know* Edward. How could this possibly be about me?"

"Suppose the killer buried him on your property because he or she wanted your business to fail?"

The glow from the dashboard lights allowed Shannon a good look at the strength shining in Melanie's eyes. It was clear she was determined to prove her innocence. Shannon didn't want to squash that, but she didn't want her friend to find hope in misguided places, either. "Now that all my family issues are resolved, I can't see that happening."

"Maybe it's not someone in your family."

"Then who?"

"What about Morgan Lombardi? She thinks you ruined a job she loved, so she has a motive to want to get back at you."

Shannon thought about the former manager of the Paisley Craft Market & Artist Lofts who she'd caught selling-off equipment from the store not long after she'd first arrived to town. "True, but by killing your ex? That seems like a drastic measure to take."

"You may not know this about her, but she was a big flirt," Melanie said. "Maybe she flirted with Ed, and he pursued her after we split up. Then, sometime later, they had a fight."

"I don't know. It sounds farfetched that he would come back to Apple Grove to look up Morgan after he'd moved to Portland."

"Maybe he was seeing her before we split."

"Wouldn't something like that get around town?"

"Not if they were careful." Melanie grabbed Shannon's arm. "C'mon, Shannon. I think it's worth pursuing."

With a start, Shannon realized she was doing the exact same thing as Grayson. She already considered Melanie the central focus of the crime. But Melanie had a point, and a *good* detective would consider all the possible motives.

Even if one of those motives turned out to be trying to ruin the Paisley Craft Market & Artist Lofts.

5

Shannon drove down Apple Grove's deserted Main Street. The businesses were all dark, lit only by the soft glow from the old-fashioned street lamps. Thick fog had drifted in from the ocean, creating an eerie feel in the usually warm and cozy town. Or maybe it was Edward's murder that had her imagination running wild.

As she approached the Paisley Craft Market, she spotted a tall man standing near the crime scene tape, staring into the big hole left by the backhoe. A thin, uniformed officer leaned against her building and watched the man's every move like a hawk.

When Shannon's headlights illuminated the man, she immediately recognized Michael and slowed her truck.

She knew she should head home and get some sleep, but she was too curious to do so. Before she convinced herself to keep driving, she whipped her truck into a parking spot and then quickly ran a hand over her unruly curls before climbing out.

Michael turned, and she took in his khakis, polo shirt, and deck shoes—so different from the dark suit and crisp white shirt he'd been wearing when she last saw him. Shannon had to suppress a smile; if her friend Coleen were with her, she'd likely point out how he looked "remarkably handsome" in her too-loud whisper. Immediately, Shannon felt a tinge of longing for her dearest friend in Scotland.

Michael watched her approach. Although his gaze appeared confident, she sometimes thought she detected a bit of uncertainty behind his bravado. It was a most intriguing contradiction.

"What brings you out here this late at night?" she asked, trying not to sound flustered by the way her pulse sped up at the sight of him.

He raised a brow. "I could ask the same thing of you."

Shannon couldn't help but feel a little irked by the way he often turned a question back at her instead of simply giving a direct answer. After the support he had offered her earlier in the day, she'd hoped his attitude toward her might have changed for good. But it looked like the Michael who didn't let anyone get too close had returned once again.

"OK then," she said, one hand on her hip. "I guess I'll have to assume that you're out here because you're perversely fascinated by gruesome discoveries."

"Aren't you?"

"*I'm* not the one standing out here staring into a hole in the ground," she snapped.

The corners of his mouth lifted slightly. "But you *are* standing here."

"Only because I was driving by and saw you studying my property, I couldn't help but wonder what you were doing." Shannon paused briefly. "Have you heard any news through the grapevine related to Edward's murder?"

Michael leaned his shoulder on the nearby street lamp. He appeared relaxed, but his sharp expression told her he was far from comfortable. "I'm not one to listen to local gossip."

"I forgot. You're more of a facts person, aren't you?"

"Facts never lie." He smiled, revealing his perfectly straight teeth.

She couldn't stop her own smile from forming … even as she silently chastised herself for allowing the exasperating man to have such a profound effect on her.

"I imagine you spent the better part of the day with Melanie," he said.

He sounded so sure of himself. The fact that his assumption was correct only added to Shannon's frustration. "I did."

"How's she doing?"

"She's coping."

"I can tell you're still worried about her," he said. "Try not to let it eat away at you. If it helps, innocent people survive investigations like this all the time."

He'd said *people* survive investigations, but his inflection on the word made Shannon wonder if he was thinking of someone in particular, someone in his current life or his past—or even himself, perhaps?

"Thanks," she said. "I'll try to keep that in mind."

"Melanie may be the prime suspect at the moment, but with all of you supporting her, I'm sure she'll come through this ordeal just fine."

Shannon pursed her lips. "If you don't listen to gossip, how did you know she's still the prime suspect?"

"Grayson likes to shoot the breeze sometimes. Since I have a law enforcement background, he often bounces theories off me."

"When you were in law enforcement, did you work homicides?" she asked.

"No."

They stared at each other in silence as she waited for him to elaborate. But he remained obstinately silent, his face impassive.

"Och! Would it kill you to give out a tiny piece of information about yourself for once? Something besides your cryptic one-syllable answers?" Shannon demanded. "I mean, you could've said, 'No, Shannon, I worked property crimes,' or 'assault,' or anything else that you did."

Surprisingly, Michael laughed, and the hearty, joyful sound irritated her even more.

"It's been awhile since I've seen that Scottish temper of yours," he said. "How about 'No, Shannon, I was in narcotics'?" He paused as his eyes lingered on hers. "If you want to know anything more about me, just ask."

He sounded sincere, but his guarded expression still gave away nothing. Did his words hold a subtle meaning? Did he *want* her to ask additional questions about him, about his past?

She was tempted to hurl an unending barrage of questions at him and discover once and for all what lurked behind those unreadable eyes of his, but she couldn't do it. The whole conversation held an undertone that was too personal to dive into so late at night. She was exhausted and didn't think she could keep up with the nuances of such a conversation. Far better to keep things strictly professional.

"Thank you for that. I'm sorry I snapped at you. It's been a long day." She cleared her throat. "Did, um, Grayson mention anything else Melanie might need to know about?"

"I'm not at liberty to say. My conversations with Grayson

are confidential," he answered. "The only reason I mentioned she was a suspect is because the officer on duty tonight felt free to share that fact with me. And that means it's public knowledge."

The chief is fortunate to have an experienced professional like Michael acting as his sounding board.

Shannon tapped her finger on her chin. "I'm wondering … could our conversations be confidential too?"

He tilted his head to the side. "Meaning?"

"Meaning if I were to ask for your advice on how to best help Melanie through this, you wouldn't share this discussion—or any future related discussions—with Grayson."

"Sure. I can keep a secret, unless it involves breaking the law. Then I'd have to rat you out." That smile again— so attractive, yet maddening at the same time.

"Thanks for the warning," she said. "Suppose you were wrongly suspected of committing this murder. How would you go about clearing your name?"

"Do you want to know what *I* would do, or what I think *you* should do?" He watched her, his gaze dark and unfathomable in the dim light.

She didn't mean to get caught up in his stare, but the man had the most captivating eyes. And even though she hadn't looked at or dated another man since her husband died, she couldn't help but think Michael *might* be interested in her as more than just a friend.

Am I reading too much into things? Not that it matters. I'm not ready to date again … am I?

"Shannon?" he asked.

She shook off her distraction and focused on the

conversation at hand. "Aren't 'what you would do' and 'what you think I should do' the very same thing?"

"Not at all. I'd start my own investigation. But I think you should leave that to the professionals."

"You think I don't have what it takes to solve this?" she asked, insulted at his tone.

He pushed off the lamppost and took a firm stance. "I think a man's been murdered, and I'd hate to see you become the killer's next target."

Shannon frowned. "So what you're saying is, if you were me, you'd step back and let the police arrest Melanie for a crime she didn't commit?"

"Come on, Shannon. You know I'm not saying that. I just ..." He shook his head. "Never mind."

She studied him, trying to assess what he wasn't saying. But all she saw was the wall he kept up, high and strong, a wall he clearly had no intention of letting down for her. She was wasting her time trying to break through it.

"It's late, I'd better get going. Thanks for your input," she said, turning to walk away. "And don't worry, I'll be careful."

"Shannon," he called after her. When she glanced back at him, he said, "Means, motive and opportunity. Find someone who has all three, and you'll be well on your way to finding the killer."

Well, that's better. The man had actually volunteered a helpful answer. Shannon allowed herself a small victory smile as she climbed into her old pickup truck.

*   *   *

Early the next morning, unable to sleep and feeling lost without the shop to open, Shannon wandered around the mansion. She stopped in the study, or, as she'd come to think of it, her craft room. The air was filled with a wonderful vanilla scent from a large three-wick candle. The lemon yellow walls and bright furnishings always lifted her mood when she stepped through the door, as did the shelves filled with crafting supplies waiting to be put to use.

Still, she sighed. She hadn't expected to feel so disoriented without a place to go first thing in the morning. It was clear the business had come to mean more to her than she'd realized. She loved the connection to her grandmother. Perhaps once she decided how to better move forward in her relationship with her own mother, the shop could foster that connection too.

Shannon's thoughts soon turned to Melanie, and she recalled Michael's parting suggestion from the previous evening, 'Means, motive and opportunity.'

So far, Melanie was the only person who met all three of Michael's criteria, though Shannon didn't think Melanie had the strength to overpower Edward and plunge a knitting needle into his neck. She assumed Grayson must be wondering the same thing. So why was he so willing to declare Melanie his main suspect?

Shannon's cellphone chimed from the table in the hallway, and when she heard the ringtone, she raced to answer it. Before Shannon had departed for America, Lara had given her a crash course in using a smartphone so they could communicate on the go. Lara had also assigned a special ringtone to her number, and now that lighthearted tune rang out from the phone.

"Sweetheart," Shannon answered, feeling almost giddy to be talking to her daughter. "I'm so glad you called. How are you? How's school? What's new?"

Lara laughed. "Slow down, Mum. One question at a time."

"Sorry. I'm just so glad to hear your voice. I miss you terribly." Shannon felt tears pricking her eyes. When she'd decided to stay in Oregon, she'd had no idea how very difficult it would be to live such a long distance from her twins.

"I miss you too." Lara drew in a deep breath, seeming to hold it and then exhaling in a long hiss.

Instantly, Shannon's stomach clutched. Lara only breathed like that when something was wrong. It had started in the third grade, the day she'd come home and had to report that she'd received detention for cutting off the ponytail of a girl she'd caught teasing Alec. Shannon knew bad news was coming.

"What's wrong, Lara?"

"Who said anything was wrong?" Lara's words were lighthearted, but the timbre of her voice was dismal.

"I'm your mother, remember? I know everything."

"I hate that you can tell I have a problem by a simple intake of air."

And Shannon was thankful for it. "Someday when you have children of your own, you'll be glad for a mother's intuition. Now, about your problem," she probed.

"It's not me, it's Alec. He's been acting moody and withdrawn all week. And before you say it's just his usual tension during exam week, it's not."

Shannon's apprehension intensified. "He's not confiding in you, and you have no idea of the cause of his behavior?"

"Exactly," Lara said. "He's never shut me out before, and I don't know what to do." Lara was right. Alec never withdrew from her. Never. So his problem had to be big.

"I'll give him a call," Shannon said.

"Would you? But don't tell him I phoned or blurt out that you know there's a problem. Wait for him to mention something."

"I'll be subtle, of course."

Lara scoffed. "C'mon, Mum, it's me, remember? Subtlety and patience are not your strong suits."

Her children knew her almost as well as she knew them. A sharp stab of loneliness sliced into Shannon's heart. She couldn't wait for summer to come so they could all be together again. "I'll do my best, sweetheart."

"Thanks—and let me know what you find out, OK?" Lara asked.

"I will. So everything's good with you, then?"

"Fine. I hate to rush off, but I have to meet up with my study group."

"Be sure to eat something before you go." Shannon clenched the phone tightly, not wanting the call to end so soon.

"I'm 19, not 6," Lara teased. Her sweet, carefree giggle brought a smile to Shannon's face.

"I love you, sweetheart."

"Love you too. Bye."

"Bye," Shannon whispered as tears stung her eyes. She hung up and immediately dialed Alec before the pain of separation took over her emotions and made her sit down for a good cry.

"This is Alec." Her son's voice sounded strong through the phone. "I can't talk now, leave a message ... and I might call you back."

Shannon waited for the beep. "Alec, it's Mum. I haven't heard from you in a while and wanted to catch up with you. Give me a call on my cellphone when you can."

She pressed "End Call" on her cellphone and walked to the front door to look out over the lush, green property. She could hardly wait until the semester ended, when she'd hop on a plane to Scotland and be reunited with the twins. Then, after packing up the house, they'd all fly back to Oregon to spend the summer together.

How glorious the summer would be! They'd play on the beach, explore the old mansion together, and cook and laugh in the kitchen, just like old times. Of course, the twins would leave again in the fall to go to Portland State. But she could handle them being a one-hour drive away a lot better than a fifteen-hour flight.

She sighed as she watched the gray clouds rolling in. Summery beach days seemed an eternity away.

A police SUV came into view as it wound its way up the long drive, and concern for Melanie sent Shannon's nostalgic feelings packing. The vehicle rolled to a stop in the circular drive, and the chief climbed out, holding several plastic bags that looked like the evidence bags Shannon had seen on television shows. She watched as he rolled them up and palmed them, then settled his hand behind his back. Judging by his behavior, she suspected one of the bags contained the knitting needle found in Edward's neck.

The time had finally come. Grayson would force her

to examine the deadly needle and possibly implicate her friend in Edward's murder. Dreading the task, she opened the door as the chief lumbered up the steps. He was a bit on the pudgy side, and by the time he reached the porch, his breathing was labored.

"Hello, Shannon," he said.

"Grayson." Shannon couldn't bring herself to muster up a warm greeting for him. "I presume you'd like to come in?"

"I would, thank you."

She led the way into the drawing room, feeling as if a week had passed since his last visit. But in reality it had only been one day.

"Have a seat," she said.

Grayson dropped into the chair Melanie had sat in the day before. "Now that you've had more time to think about Ed's death, I was wondering if you'd come up with any information that might help us solve this case," he said.

"I'm afraid not."

"And what about Melanie? Has she had any ideas?"

Shannon shrugged. "You'll have to ask her. I haven't spoken to her this morning. She's working at The Flower Pot right now."

Grayson raised a bushy eyebrow. "Why do I get the feeling you're trying to stonewall my investigation?"

"I'm not stonewalling," Shannon said. "I don't want to speak for Melanie."

He watched her for a moment. Then he brought his hand from behind his back in dramatic fashion and unfurled the bags like a red carpet at a grand ball. But there was nothing joyous or grand about the situation.

"I mentioned that I would like you to look at the needle taken from Ed's body," Grayson said. He sorted through the bags and handed one to her. "What can you tell me about this?"

Shannon placed the clear bag on her lap and schooled her expression so she wouldn't instantly broadcast how she felt about whatever she discovered. Then she moved the bag a bit so she could clearly see the connector. Each needle manufacturer used unique connectors to attach long circular cables to their needles, and she should be able to identify the maker from the connecter.

She poked the stainless steel, turning it around to examine it, and her heart sank. She lifted the bag and gave the needle another close look. It was a Get-the-Point brand needle, size ten. A size commonly found in the manufacturer's circular set ... and a set identical to the one Melanie had recently purchased at the Paisley Craft Market.

"Shannon," Grayson said, causing her to jump. "You've memorized every bit of that needle by now. Care to share what you know?"

"It's a Get-the-Point brand needle," she replied, determined to offer only the barest of information.

"Do you sell this brand in your shop?"

She swallowed. "Yes."

"So someone may have bought this from you?"

"Possibly."

"Do you keep track of who buys specific items?"

"We do keep records about special-order items, but not items we regularly stock, and this is part of our regular inventory." She paused to consider her words, carefully trying to not implicate Melanie but making sure she told the truth.

"It's a popular brand of interchangeable needles."

"Can you explain the 'interchangeable' part to me?"

Shannon nodded. "It would be easier to demonstrate. Let me grab a set to show you." She all but tossed the offending needle at him as she stood and hurried to her craft room, thankful to have a private moment to calm her frayed nerves. She pulled open the drawer holding her assortment of needles and selected a circular set. As she trudged back to the drawing room, she couldn't help but feel a little like a prisoner walking to the gallows.

She forced a smile, figuring it might help set the chief at ease. "I'm guessing you don't want to know *why* we use this kind of needle, but how they work. Is that right?"

"Correct."

She opened the cloth case and selected two number ten needles. Then she demonstrated snapping the bamboo tips onto the cables. "We cast on the stitches like a regular needle and start knitting."

He held up the evidence bag. "This needle is metal, but yours looks like it's made of something else."

"Mine is bamboo, but tips can be made of many different materials, such as aluminum, stainless, wood, or plastic."

He pointed at her case. "But it's likely that this needle is part of a set similar to that one?"

"Most likely. You can purchase the tips and cables separately, but the beauty of owning an interchangeable set is that you can change sizes and cable lengths as needed."

"And your friend Melanie. Does she have a set like this?" Grayson asked.

Shannon's heart started to gallop. She couldn't say

no, but she wouldn't come out and say yes either. "It's not uncommon for die-hard knitters like Melanie to own a set, or several sets even."

His eyes narrowed. "Did she buy a set like this in your shop?"

"Like I said, we don't keep records of in-stock purchases." Shannon felt a bead of sweat run down the back of her neck. Her guilt about being evasive threatened to derail her calm facade, but she managed to tamp the feeling down.

All Grayson would need to do to get a straight answer to his question is ask Melanie if she owned a Get-the-Point set. Once she admitted that she did, Shannon was sure he'd demand to know if she was missing the number ten needle from that set—which was exactly what Shannon planned to ask Melanie the moment Grayson was out of her hair.

— 6 —

The old blue truck left a thick trail of exhaust as Shannon sped down Main Street. She absently returned the friendly waves from people she knew, her mind focused on her mission: Get to Melanie before the chief. Since she couldn't get her on the phone, Shannon only hoped that she'd driven fast enough to beat Grayson to The Flower Pot so she could warn Melanie of his impending visit.

Not likely, though. Sitting behind a steering wheel on the left side of a vehicle still flustered Shannon when she hurried. Never mind trying to drive on the right side of the road.

She spotted The Flower Pot's brightly striped awning gleaming in a sunny break and stepped harder on the gas. With worry for her friend nagging at her, Shannon angled her truck into the first available spot and jumped out. She quickly surveyed the quiet street for any sign of a police vehicle, but spotted none.

Good, maybe I've arrived before Grayson.

She raced up the sidewalk to the large picture window that featured a mixture of dazzling floral arrangements. Her heart swelled with pride for Melanie, who'd created the breathtaking displays of cut flowers herself.

As Shannon pushed through the front door of the shop, a small bell tinkled from above, announcing her arrival.

The strong smell of fragrant flowers did nothing to ease her concern as she searched among the large containers of brilliantly colored flowers until she spotted Elaina Garret, the owner of the shop, talking with a man Shannon didn't recognize.

Elaina, who was in her early 30s, wore her shoulder-length hair scraped back from her face in a ponytail most of the time. But this morning, it was loose and softly flowing around her face. She gazed up at the man standing next to her with adoration.

Shannon rushed over to join them. "Is Melanie working today?" she demanded.

"Shannon, hi," Elaina said, raising her brows at Shannon's sharp tone. "Yes, Mel's in the cooler, picking out some flowers. She should be right out."

"Thank goodness." Shannon blew out a long breath and felt her shoulders slump.

"You seem upset. Is something wrong?"

"Um, no. I just really need to talk to her." Shannon shoved her shaking hands into the pockets of her skirt to hide them. Then she forced a tremulous smile.

Elaina's face softened. "No problem."

The man hovering nearby cleared his throat and took a step closer before placing a possessive hand on Elaina's shoulder.

"Oh, sorry." Elaina smiled an apology at him before returning her focus to Shannon. "Allow me to introduce my boyfriend, Randy Parson."

"It's a pleasure to meet you, Shannon." Randy held out his hand and offered a warm smile.

"You too." Shannon reluctantly pulled her trembling

hand from her pocket. As they shook, she could see how Elaina would be attracted to him. Tall and on the thin side, he was quite handsome when he smiled.

"I've been meaning to get over to your shop and welcome you to town," he said, releasing her hand. "I'm a photographer, and I'd hoped to display some of my pictures in your new coffee shop addition—when it's completed."

"Randy took all of the photos on that wall." Elaina's voice rang with pride as she gestured toward framed scenes of the Oregon coast that were displayed behind the front counter.

Shannon studied the pictures. She recognized the famous spots, like Haystack Rock, Cape Kiwanda, and Tillamook Rock Lighthouse. He'd shot the photos in various lights, and they were stunning. "Do you do this as a hobby, or is it a business?" she asked.

"Business. At Coastal Photos, we reproduce the photos you see here, and I sell them at gift shops up and down the coast. Plus, I have a booming online business too." Randy pulled back his shoulders. "We print upwards of half a million pictures a year."

He sounded so proud of his accomplishment, Shannon hated to have to tell him no—artists suffered enough disappointments without her adding to them. "Though your photos are amazing, I'm really looking for one-of-a-kind items to display in Espresso Yourself," she said.

His easy smile disappeared in a flash, and he seemed to look at her in a new light. "Oh, sorry. I must've misunderstood what you were looking for."

"That said, I'd love to display any unique photos that you've taken. They would help raise money for our charities."

"Yeah, I might do that," he said, but he didn't sound very convincing.

Elaina tsked and plucked at his shirtsleeve. "C'mon. You have some amazing pictures at your house that you could show." Elaina looked at Shannon again. "I'll help him pick out a few and bring them over for you to see."

"Sounds great." Though Shannon liked Elaina and normally would have been happy to chat with her and her boyfriend, she could feel the minutes ticking by. She feared Grayson would burst through the front door at any minute. "Would it be OK if I go back and find Melanie?"

"We can do that for you," Randy offered. "It will give the two of us a few minutes alone before I have to head into work." He winked at Elaina, and grabbed her hand, tugging her toward the back room. "Nice meeting you, Shannon."

Shannon tried to wait patiently for Melanie, but her foot tapped as she kept watch out the window for Grayson. She'd expected him to head straight to the shop, but other business must have interfered.

"Shannon?" Melanie called out to her from behind.

Shannon whirled. "Oh, Mel. Thank goodness!"

Melanie stood in the doorway to the back rooms, her arms laden with flowers. "What's wrong?" she asked, gently setting the flowers on the counter.

"It's Grayson. He showed me the needle used to kill Edward." Shannon paused to slow her agitated breathing. "It's from a Get-the-Point set like yours."

"So?" Melanie did not appear at all concerned by the news as she began to separate the flowers into neat piles on the counter. "They're one of your best sellers, right? I'm not the only one in town who uses them."

Shannon didn't want to upset her friend, but she had to make Melanie see how dire the news was. "But you're the only one who the chief believes had a motive to kill Ed."

"It's no big deal. I'll show him that I have all my needles. They're in my car." She wiped her hands on her striped apron and then took it off. "Let me tell Elaina I'm taking my break, and then I'll go get them." Melanie pulled out her bag from under the counter, dug out her keys, and disappeared into the back room.

Shannon stepped outside to wait and rolled her shoulders, hoping to force tense muscles to relax. *What's going on here?* She was usually the levelheaded one, and Melanie was the one who was a bit flighty. But just now, her friend had kept her cool, logically reasoning how to prove the killer hadn't used her needle, while Shannon fluttered about like the sky was falling.

Pull it together, Shannon. This is no time to fall apart.

Glancing around, she spotted Melanie's vehicle parked a few spaces down the street and she began to stroll toward it, keeping her eyes open for any sign of Grayson. A lone police vehicle parked at the end of the block near the Pink Sprinkles Bakery caught her eye, but most of the Apple Grove officers drove the same type of SUV, so she couldn't tell if it was Grayson's vehicle or if it belonged to another officer. A renewed feeling of unease settled over her as she scanned her surroundings for any sign of him.

The locks on Melanie's doors clicked open, and Shannon turned to see her friend approaching with her key fob pointed at her SUV. She hurried to the back of the vehicle, lifted the hatchback door, and dug through her knitting bag. Pulling out a brightly patterned cloth case, she untied the long tabs and unrolled it. "See all of them are …" Her head popped up, and her mouth fell open.

"One of them is missing." Shannon said it so low that she didn't know if Melanie had heard.

"But *how*?" Melanie whispered, her face paling as it had the day they'd found Edward's body.

"Someone stole it, that's how." Shannon searched the empty slot and confirmed the missing needle was a number ten.

"I don't know when they could have gotten it. My knitting is always with me." Melanie clutched her chest, her eyes wide and fearful.

"Except during times like this, when you're inside the shop and it's in your car. Or when you go for your nightly walk."

Melanie sucked in a breath. "Oh my gosh, you're right!"

"When did you last use the number ten set?" Shannon asked.

Melanie's mouth opened and closed a few times but no sound came out.

Shannon wrapped her arm around her friend's shoulder. "It's OK, take your time," she said.

"I don't know, I just don't know." Melanie fanned her face as if she might pass out. "They're really going to think I did it. I'm going to jail."

"Not if I can help it," Shannon said, pulling her friend closer. Looking down the street, she tried to come up with their next move. She caught sight of Michael's security business—the silver shield emblem for Stone & McCrary on the glass door glinted in the sunlight like a beacon of hope.

Michael would know what to do in such a difficult situation. Maybe he'll help us.

Shannon eased Melanie into a sitting position on the bumper. "Wait here," she said. Then she ran across the road. She pushed on the door of Michael's business, but it was locked. Not unusual—Michael often worked from home.

She hurried back to Melanie, who still sat woodenly on the bumper. Shannon couldn't let Grayson question her friend in her current state.

"Let's go to your place and see if we can prove someone broke into your house to steal the needle," she said, helping Melanie to her feet. "I've got Michael's number in my cellphone, so I'll call him on the way. Perhaps he can tell us what to look for."

"OK. Fine," Melanie agreed, sounding dazed.

Shannon gently pried the keys from her friend's hand and settled her into the passenger seat. Then she dialed Michael on her cellphone as she ran around the front of the car.

"This is Stone." His deep voice resonated through the phone.

"Michael, it's Shannon. I'm so glad I caught you." She explained Melanie's dilemma while she climbed behind the wheel. "I'm putting you on speaker so I can drive while we talk. Melanie will hold the phone."

Shannon held the phone out to Melanie, who sat staring blankly out the window. "Mel?"

Melanie absently grabbed the phone and held it up between them.

"So, Michael," Shannon said as she backed onto the road, "other than the usual marks from a door or window being forced open, what else should we look for?"

He sighed. "Rather than try and explain everything, it would be easier if I come over to Melanie's house and take a look myself."

Shannon felt a glimmer of hope. "Would you mind?"

"I'll be there in ten minutes."

"Thank you." Shannon took a quick look at Melanie and saw that some of her color had returned. "You can end the call now, Mel."

"Oh, sorry." Melanie seemed to snap out of her daze as she disconnected the call and set the phone in the cup holder.

"I'm glad I thought to call him," Shannon said. "He should be a big help."

"Yeah." Melanie wrinkled her nose at Shannon and a hint of a smile played on her lips. "Now, if only you can manage to keep your mind on the missing needle and not on him."

"W-what?"

Melanie rolled her eyes. "Oh, come on, Shannon. You're not fooling any of us. We see the way you look at him."

"The way I look at him? What are you talking about?" Shannon was still stunned by Melanie's comment.

Melanie playfully punched Shannon's arm. "Relax. It's a good thing."

Shannon fired a horrified look at her friend. "No it's not, Mel. Even if I *was* looking for a relationship—and I'm not saying I am—you know how secretive and closed off Michael is. What kind of relationship could I possibly hope to have with a man like that?"

"I've known him for a long time," Melanie said. "He's a good guy.

"But no one can know everything about another person. Your ex is a perfect example of that," Shannon pointed out. "You thought you knew him, and then he bailed on you during the worst time of your life."

"Michael's not like that."

"Well, just for the record, I am not 'looking' at Michael. In fact, I barely even notice the man." Shannon raised her chin, her tone a warning to Melanie that the topic was closed to further discussion.

Melanie raised her eyebrows, but said nothing.

Shannon swung the car into Melanie's driveway. "Why don't you look around inside to see if you notice anything odd you may have missed before?" Shannon said. "I'll check your doors and windows."

"I'm so glad you're my friend." Melanie's voice trembled as if she might cry.

Shannon hugged Melanie. "Me too, Mel."

They climbed the steps to the front porch of Melanie's small beach cottage. Bright white with a powder blue front door and window trim, the home had a perfect view of the ocean. Shannon turned to watch the waves roll in and out while Melanie unlocked the door.

"I don't see any pry marks by the lock," Melanie observed before stepping inside.

Shannon squatted down to eye level and made a thorough inspection of the lock and the painted wood surrounding it. Melanie was right. Not a bit of evidence of a break-in.

Shannon circled the exterior, performing the same inspection of the windows, the back door, and the garage door. But she found nothing amiss.

What are we missing?

Shannon wandered through the house in search of her friend. She found her in the living room, staring at a large stone fireplace surrounded by white knotty pine paneling.

"I doubt he came down the chimney, like Santa," Shannon said.

Melanie looked up and smiled, but it was half-hearted.

Shannon joined her near the fireplace, catching a faint whiff of charred wood and ashes as she approached. "Did Edward still have a key to your house?"

"He wasn't supposed to, but I wouldn't put it past him to have one made before he returned his to me."

Shannon thought for a moment. "So whoever killed him could've gotten the key from him before the attack."

"I suppose. If that's the case, then I'll never be able to prove someone broke in, and Grayson will continue to think I'm the killer." Melanie walked to the window and pressed her forehead against the glass. "Michael's here. I sure hope he has some ideas."

Through the glass, Shannon watched Michael emerge from his car. Dressed in khakis and a long-sleeved denim shirt, he strode confidently toward the house, his eyes assessing his surroundings as he moved. He appeared agile and sure on his feet. Shannon suspected the confidence he exuded gave his clients strong peace of mind.

"Um, Shannon," Melanie said. Shannon pried her eyes off Michael to look at her friend. "Would you mind letting him in?"

"Of course." Shannon hurried to unlock the door. When she opened it, she found Michael's hand in the air, poised to knock. "Thanks for coming."

"No problem." He didn't look at her but instead ran a finger over the lock. "Did you find any signs of a forced entry?"

"No," she said. "I'm wondering if whoever stole the needle might've had a key."

His head popped up. "Are you sure it was taken from the house?"

"Well, no."

"Then I'd like to talk to Melanie about it before looking around."

"Sure." Shannon stepped back, and as he passed, she caught a hint of the minty soap she'd come to associate with him.

His footsteps pounded on the wooden floor as he crossed the room and joined Melanie near the window.

"Would you mind answering a few questions for me?" he asked her gently.

Melanie shook her head and gestured at the blue plaid sofa. "Please, have a seat."

Michael perched on the edge and Shannon sat nearby in a worn club chair. Melanie remained stiffly rooted in place.

"How certain are you that the needle you're missing was taken from your home?" Michael asked.

"I really don't know for sure," Melanie said. "I mean, I think it was. I usually only take my knitting a few places. To the Craft Market for our knitting group … and to work, on the days when Elaina is off and I have to watch the shop during my lunch break."

Warming up to the discussion, Shannon leaned forward in her chair. "Can you recall the last time you used the set of needles?" she asked.

"No, but I know it's been a while." Melanie looked up at the ceiling, pondering the question. "A month or more, maybe. But that's only a guess."

"And in that time, was your knitting ever left unattended in your car?" Michael asked.

"I suppose so—for brief periods of time."

"Your car could've easily been accessed with a slim-jim," he said. "It doesn't take a lot of skill or knowledge to use one to pop open a lock, and you wouldn't be able to detect it."

"Except that anytime the knitting's in Melanie's car, it's during the day, and she's in town. Right, Mel?" Shannon asked.

Melanie nodded. "Most of the time, anyway."

"Any intruder would easily be seen," Shannon added.

Michael sat forward on the sofa. "Can you think of a time in the last month when it could've been in your car, but your car was parked in a place *not* easily seen by others?"

"Um ..." Melanie tapped a finger against her chin. "Once. About three weeks ago, when Elaina was out of town, and I took over for her at The Flower Pot. I parked in her spot in the alley that day."

"Maybe that's when the needle was taken." Shannon's enthusiasm for a potential lead bubbled into her words.

"Three weeks ago, I'm not so sure," Michael said cautiously. "If I'd planned to use the needle to kill someone, I wouldn't take it and then wait three weeks to use it. Too many chances during that time for Melanie to discover it missing."

Melanie lifted her hands in surrender. "Then I guess it had to be taken from here."

"And since there's no sign of forced entry, that means the thief either has a key or is very adept at picking locks," Michael said, looking from Shannon to Melanie, his expression deadly serious. "It also means our killer is a calculating individual, and the murder was premeditated. That kind of guy isn't someone either of you should mess around with."

"But we have to clear my name!" Melanie cried out. "It's obvious Grayson isn't going to; he already has me convicted in his mind."

"We don't know that," Michael said. "Look, Grayson might be a control freak and a little over the top sometimes, but he's also an excellent cop. I'm confident he'll find the real killer. You have to give him time to do his job."

Shannon met Michael's gaze and tried to telegraph that they had no time. If the investigation continued to turn up evidence that pointed to Melanie, then Grayson would soon arrest her. And Shannon couldn't let her friend go to jail. Not even if the killer was as dangerous as Michael feared.

— 7 —

Later that afternoon, Shannon parked her truck in front of Apple Grove's senior center. Between Melanie's impending conversation with Grayson and Alec's failure to return her call, she knew the day would continue to hold stress.

And that meant baking. Lots of baking.

However, if she wanted to bake even one more cookie, she had to find a home for the items overflowing from her pantry and refrigerator. She'd taught crafting classes at the senior center, and she knew she'd find plenty of hungry crafters there, late in the afternoon.

But first, she needed to make a call. She took out her cellphone, tempted to call Alec again, but then decided she'd be patient and wait a day for him to return her call before checking in with him. Melanie was another story. Before she'd left Melanie's house, she'd made her friend promise to call and report in if Grayson stopped by. Melanie still hadn't called, and Shannon was sure he would've been there by now.

She dialed Melanie's number and waited for her to pick up. Through her truck window, she watched as several older residents exited the center and headed for their cars. On the fifth ring, Melanie answered.

"Did the chief come over to see you yet?" Shannon asked, wasting no time with a greeting.

"Not yet." Only two words, but Shannon could hear the dread in her friend's tone.

"You shouldn't be alone. I'll come over and wait with you."

"Thank you, but no." Melanie's voice was firm. "Like I said before, we have no idea if or when Grayson will drop by, and I don't want to keep intruding on your time."

"But with the shop still closed, I'm not doing anything except dropping off goodies at the senior center," Shannon protested.

Melanie's gentle laugh rippled through the phone. "If you don't find something else to keep you busy, you're going to fatten up the whole town."

Shannon wished beading occupied her mind the way baking did, but while beadwork fulfilled her creative needs, it didn't keep her mind from wandering to her problems. "Are you sure you don't want me to come over?" she asked.

"Positive. I promise I'll call you when I have something to report."

"OK. Talk to you later." Shannon hung up. She should have been happy that Melanie had overcome her fear and now felt as if she could handle being alone. But the worry she felt for her friend lingered as she climbed out of the truck and ran around to the passenger side to grab a tray of cookies. Her hair whipped in the strong ocean winds, and she shivered. Fighting to keep the tray from flying away, she made her way to the front door and pushed it open with her backside.

Women seated in chairs before a blazing fireplace directed a chorus of hellos her way. The knitting class, led by Betty, was in full swing. Shannon smiled as she met her friend's sparkling blue eyes. Though only in her mid-50s, Betty had joined the senior center so she could use their fitness equipment. But what she'd discovered was a wonderful group of women close to her age who enjoyed many of the same hobbies she liked and a place where she could escape the stresses of running the Apple Grove Inn.

Betty set her knitting needles on the chair, excused herself from the class, and approached Shannon. "I figured after everything you served yesterday, you'd be bringing goodies over here," said Betty, taking the tray of cookies. "Want help getting the rest?"

"I can handle it, thanks." Shannon returned to the truck, noting how the winds kept the bright red flags near the entrance fluttering. Today would be a perfect day to fly kites at the beach, and Shannon couldn't help but wish that Alec and Lara were with her to do so.

By the time she reentered the building, Betty had set up a table, and the coffee pot was gurgling. The aroma of freshly brewed java easily overpowered the center's heavy strawberry-scented air freshener.

Shannon set the trays of sweets on the table. "Thanks for setting this up on the spur of the moment," she said to Betty.

"No problem. Everyone around here loves home-baked goodies." Betty's eyes darkened with intensity. "Too bad all of these wonderful treats mean you're still worried about something. Is this about Melanie?"

"Partially."

"And the other part?"

Shannon was reluctant to share her concerns about Alec; she knew she could simply be overreacting. On the other hand, with grown children of her own, Betty might understand, and maybe she could help.

"It's Alec," Shannon blurted, taking Betty by the arm and directing her to a private alcove. "Lara says something's bothering him, and she can't get him to talk about it. I tried calling him but got his voice mail."

"And you're worried it's something serious?"

"Yes, this behavior isn't like him. He's always been easygoing and good spirited. He's never cut himself off from Lara like he's doing now. They have a very strong twin connection."

Betty's expression softened in an understanding way only a mother could know. "Being his mother, you want to hop on the next plane to Scotland and rescue him."

"Exactly. Or … I could ask Coleen to go talk to him."

Betty tilted her head to the side. "You honestly think that'd go over well with a young man in college?"

"Not likely. But I'm worried. I can't sit around doing nothing, waiting for him to call me."

"Look, Shannon." Betty leaned closer. "You're used to being able to fix your kids' problems, but once they leave home, you have to back off and give them space. No matter how hard it is or how much it hurts, you have to let them fly on their own until they ask for help."

Shannon knew Betty had the right answer, but she didn't like hearing it. "I wanted you to tell me to go ahead and call Coleen. Why *must* you be so practical?"

"Sorry." Betty's full lips tipped in a smile. "I'm trying to help you do this the easy way rather than the clingy hard way, like I did."

"Then you had better get eating, because I'll be delivering more baked goods very soon," Shannon teased as she slipped her arm into Betty's and dragged her back to the refreshment table.

Shannon stayed a few minutes longer to chat with some of the women she knew. Then she drove home and headed straight to the kitchen. After brewing a cup of tea, she pulled out her recipe for thumbprint cookies and got to work.

Hours later, she massaged her lower back and took a break to admire the sea of colorfully frosted cookies covering the island. She glanced at the clock, surprised to see it was after seven—and she still hadn't heard from Melanie.

Shannon dialed her friend's number and turned on the phone's speaker. Then she started cleaning up her baking mess.

"Hello," Melanie answered, sounding sleepy.

"Did I wake you?"

"No. I'm zoned out in front of the television to take my mind off of things."

Shannon cringed. "Sorry to bring it all back up, but you never called, and I was wondering what Grayson said to you."

"He never came to see me."

"Really? I wonder why not."

"I don't know, but I'm glad he didn't, so I'm not questioning it," Melanie said with a heavy sigh, causing Shannon to feel even guiltier for bringing up the subject. "Do you mind if we don't talk about this tonight? I think I'm going to take a long soak in the tub and then go to bed."

The last thing Shannon wanted to do was drop the subject, but she respected her friend's wishes. "No problem," she said. "Sleep tight, and I'll talk to you in the morning."

Shannon hung up and absentmindedly wiped the countertop.

What could Grayson be up to? There would be no reason for him not to ask Melanie if he could see her needle set, would there? Of course, as Michael had told Melanie earlier, she could always refuse to show it to Grayson, but then he'd become even more suspicious of her. And he *could* get a warrant to see it if he wanted to, so there was no point in antagonizing him.

Shannon took the mixing bowl to the sink and sank it below a thick layer of suds. As she stuck her hands under the hot water, she couldn't help but think Melanie must be feeling like the mixing bowl—like she was sinking and the whole world was closing in around her. Like she was moments from arrest for a murder she didn't commit.

Shannon swished water over caked-on cookie dough and forced her mind off Grayson's impending visit to Melanie. Worrying for her friend would do no good. Shannon could do nothing more tonight other than pray that Melanie wouldn't find herself in even more hot water when morning broke.

* * *

Shannon pulled into the alley behind the craft market and rushed through the drizzly rain and morning fog to the back entrance. Once inside the store, she searched the space for Grayson, but she spotted only Essie, working behind the front counter.

Grayson had phoned an hour earlier, telling Shannon she could reopen the shop as usual, and that he would stop in to meet with her later. As a result, she'd immediately called Essie to tell her to come to work, and on the way in, she'd phoned the Purls to give them the good news about the store reopening. They were all eager to meet at their regularly scheduled time—all except for Melanie. She hadn't even answered, and that left Shannon worried for her friend. After Shannon talked with Grayson, she planned to head over to The Flower Pot to check up on her.

Making her way down the main aisle, Shannon noticed that a residue of fine black powder coated many items. She recognized it as the chemical used for fingerprinting. She and Essie would need to get the powdery substance cleaned up before it mixed with and ruined numerous skeins of yarn.

Essie looked up from paperwork she'd been filing. "Hi! I'm so glad we finally got the place back," she said. "It looks like it will need a thorough cleaning, though."

Shannon tried to remain optimistic with all the work waiting to be done surrounding them. "I wonder if we should wait for Grayson's approval to get started. He's not hiding out somewhere in here, is he?"

"I haven't seen him." The bells above the front door tinkled, and Essie's gaze swung to the door.

Melanie, dressed in dark jeans and a waterproof coat, stepped into the store. She shook off the rain and then pushed back her hood. "I didn't think I'd see you two here," she said as she crossed over to them. "I guess that means the investigators are done with this place."

Shannon and Essie exchanged confused looks.

"If you weren't expecting us to be here, then why did you come by?" Shannon asked.

"Grayson asked me to meet him here." Melanie smiled and casually looked around, as if on a social call. "Did he say if they've found anything in their search?"

"No. I figured he'd tell me in person," Shannon replied, perplexed by her friend's carefree demeanor.

"There he is." Essie tipped her head toward the door, her ringlet curls bouncing as she moved. "I don't suppose he'll want me hanging around, so I'll get started cleaning in the back and leave you to talk to him."

"Thanks, Essie," Shannon said. She was touched by the consideration Essie always displayed. She'd really lucked out the day Essie stopped in, looking for work. Not only were Essie's chalk drawing courses bringing in revenue, but she was an excellent manager and a great partner in Shannon's beading crafts as well.

"Ladies." Grayson greeted them as he removed his hat and shook off the rain on the front doormat. "Glad to see you both made it."

"So did you find any sign of foul play in here or not?" Shannon demanded.

"I'm not at liberty to say." As Grayson moved closer, he ran a hand over his thinning hair, settling the few remaining strands in place. "As I'm sure you saw on your way in, we've removed all crime scene tape from the property. You can resume business as usual, including the construction of your coffee shop addition."

"After leaving this place such a mess, the least you could do is tell us what you found," Shannon muttered, running a finger through the film of black powder on her countertop. The residue clung to her skin like baby powder.

"Sorry about that. Lifting fingerprints can be messy, but it's a necessary part of the investigation." Grayson offered a rare smile. "Unfortunately, budget doesn't allow the forensics team to clean up after themselves."

"Is there any news on the forensics front that you *can* share?" Shannon pressed. She held her breath and waited for him to comment on the knitting needle.

"Actually ..." He paused and took a few steps closer, as if someone might overhear them. "Yes, there is a new development I can share. According to the medical examiner, there's been a change in the cause of death."

Melanie's hand flew to her chest. "I don't understand. Ed didn't die from a knitting needle?"

"No." Grayson paused again. This time Shannon suspected he was doing it to be melodramatic. "He was poisoned."

"Poisoned!" Melanie exclaimed. "What kind of poison?"

"We don't know yet, but the medical examiner has requested additional bloodwork that will hopefully clear up the confusion."

"Oh, how terrible," Melanie said. "Did Ed suffer? I mean, was it one of those horrible poisons that you hear about on television?"

"I'm afraid I don't have that kind of information," Grayson said.

As Shannon worked to process the shocking news, she moved closer to her friend, hoping to impart strength. "As much as I hate to hear about how he died, this should at least clear Melanie's name."

The chief arched a brow, but said nothing.

"What?" Shannon asked.

"I can see how you might think that would be the case, but I'm not inclined to agree," he said.

"But I don't know *anything* about poisons." Melanie's pitch rose with each word.

"In today's world, information about poison is easy to come by on the Internet." The police chief observed Melanie with renewed suspicion. "And, truth be told, I'd wondered how a woman of your size could overpower a big man like Ed and stab him with the needle. But if he were poisoned first—"

"Why use the needle at all then?" Shannon interrupted. "That doesn't even make sense."

"I'm of the opinion it was done as a personal attack," he said. "To vent rage against the victim." Grayson fixed Melanie with another pointed look. "It's not farfetched to think an estranged spouse might want to vent a little rage."

"It's also possible the real killer intended to set up Melanie by planting one of her knitting needles in Ed's neck," Shannon pointed out.

Grayson's eyebrows shot up. "So now you *do* think the needle is one of hers?"

Shannon sucked in a breath—she'd blown it. She'd just given Grayson incriminating information against Melanie that he'd yet to determine on his own. Her gaze darted to Melanie who returned her look with a sympathetic one.

Shannon quickly decided her best plan of attack would be to change the subject. "I should hope by now you've identified more than one suspect," she challenged.

Grayson scowled. "Are you fishing for names, Shannon?"

"No. But I want to hear that you're looking at all avenues."

"I am indeed."

"Good, because I'm sure Melanie isn't the only person in the area who was not on friendly terms with Edward," Shannon said, even though she still didn't have any other names to offer.

The bells over the door chimed again and Shannon glanced behind her. Michael stood on the mat, his jacket dripping and his ebony hair shining from the clinging moisture. His gaze shifted from person to person, as if assessing the situation he'd walked into. Shannon suspected the behavior was a holdover from his days as a cop.

"Am I early?" he asked Grayson.

"No." The chief motioned for Michael to come closer. "I'll be finished here in a minute. I was about to tell Melanie that we've learned Ed received numerous threatening texts from his girlfriend's former boyfriend. It seems the ex was jealous and wanted to get back with her."

"*Finally!*" Shannon exclaimed, causing Melanie to jump. "A solid lead."

Grayson kept his attention on Melanie. "I'm on my way to talk with your son about this, but if you give us your take on it, maybe we won't have to question him. I know he's upset over the loss of his father."

Shannon saw right through Grayson's ploy. He was trying to play Melanie, and get her to lower her guard. The flash of annoyance on Michael's face confirmed her suspicion. Grayson intended to talk to Greg no matter what Melanie said.

"Greg's a strong man. He can better tell you about Ed's life since we split," Melanie replied, easily evading the chief's trap. "I had no contact with Ed, and Greg and I rarely talked about him."

"Because you and Ed had an acrimonious relationship?" Grayson suggested.

Melanie simply stared at him.

"OK." He settled his hat back on his head. "Then I guess I'll need to talk to your son. Maybe he'll know who ransacked your ex-husband's apartment." He watched them closely, as if expecting them to react.

Shannon couldn't fake surprise, and Melanie didn't seem to be able to either.

"Ah, I see you all already know about that," Grayson said. "Might it be because it was you who tore the place up searching for something?"

"That's absurd. It was that way when we got there," Melanie said, playing right into his hands. She quickly covered her mouth, and a gleam of satisfaction glinted in Grayson's eyes.

Shannon caught the flash of surprise on Michael's face, which quickly turned to irritation—focused on her. It was the one part of her investigation she hadn't shared with him.

"We went over to Ed's apartment with Greg," Melanie rushed on. "He needed to locate Angie's phone number so he could tell her what happened before she heard it on the news. He called the local police to report the break-in. You can check with them if you don't believe me."

"I intend to." Grayson started to walk away, then turned back. "I don't suppose you'd allow me to look at your set of interchangeable needles?"

"I don't suppose she would," Shannon interjected, clutching her friend closer.

Grayson shook his head at Shannon. "I understand your desire to protect Melanie, but if you get in the way of my investigation, you'll wish you hadn't. Do I make myself clear?"

Shannon wanted to argue, but a look of warning from Michael told her that arguing would only rile Grayson more, which might cause him to take it out on Melanie.

"Quite," she said.

"Stone, let's talk outside." Grayson jerked his head toward the door.

Michael gave a solemn nod. "I'll catch up with you later, Shannon."

She watched both men walk out the door and silently prayed that Michael would keep his promise to her and not mention anything they'd discussed earlier pertaining to the case. If he did break his promise and reveal any of their previous discussions, she feared Melanie would soon be arrested for murder.

8

Betty, Joyce and Kate soon joined Shannon and Melanie
at the shop, and they all slipped into the circle of chairs in
the back of the store that they normally occupied for their
Purls of Hope gatherings. Shannon served tea and coffee
that Essie had brewed in the workroom, along with a large
plate of thumbprint cookies baked the night before.

For the first time that week, Shannon felt like life was
somewhat normal. None of the ladies bothered to retrieve
their baskets filled with current knitting projects. Instead,
they decided to catch up for a few minutes, and then they
would all pitch in to help clean up the mess left by the
crime scene investigators.

Shannon blew on her mug of Earl Grey tea and
glanced at the large green tarp hanging from the ceiling.
She recalled the day her contractor had hung it to keep
construction dust out of the store as they worked on the
new coffee shop addition. It had been such a thrilling day.
Now, she couldn't help but think of the blue tarp holding
Edward's body every time she looked at it.

"You're a million miles away, Shannon," Betty said as
she cupped her usual mug of black coffee in her hands.

"Sorry." Shannon smiled. "I was thinking about how
great it will be once the addition is completed."

Joyce set down her mug and took a thumbprint cookie

with bright yellow frosting in the middle. "When will you resume work on it?"

"I've left a message for the contractor. I'm hoping he can get his crew back here tomorrow." Shannon sipped her tea, savoring the delicate flavor and the company of her friends.

"You're not wasting any time," Kate said, staring longingly at the plate of cookies.

"I thought about waiting," Shannon said, "but then I figured the sooner we build over that hole in the ground, the sooner people will forget what happened there."

Melanie had been chewing a cookie, and she swallowed hard. "Do you think finding Ed out there will taint people's opinion of the coffee shop for very long?"

"No. Maybe at first, but it will pass. You know nothing can stop a true Oregonian from getting the best coffee around." Shannon forced a laugh

"Don't I know it." Betty took a long sip of her coffee then grimaced. "No offense to Essie, but she's clearly not a coffee drinker," she whispered.

"No worries, Betty," Kate interjected. "If Shannon keeps up the marathon baking, you'll always have something at hand to sweeten your coffee with." She reached for a cookie, but then changed her mind and pulled her hand back to sit on it.

"Speaking of baking," Betty said, turning to Shannon, "did you ever sort things out with Alec?"

"Alec?" the others asked in unison.

Shannon didn't want to burden them all with her problems. But sharing her dilemma *would* get them talking about something other than murder, so she spilled her story about

Alec. "I'm going to call him again when we finish up here."

"Why wait?" Joyce shifted in her chair. The light caught the colorful gems she'd added to her jean jacket. If there was a way to adhere sparkly gems to an object, Joyce would find it. "It's clear you're worried about him, and we can handle the cleanup ourselves."

Shannon shook her head. "I don't want to move. It feels so good to be together like this again and temporarily forget about the grim reality of what happened outside on the lawn."

"I, for one, can't forget that easily," Melanie said, scowling. "Especially not with the fingerprint mess all around us."

"Why don't we get started cleaning?" Kate jumped up, giving the plate of cookies one last evil glare. "We can talk as we work, and Shannon, you can call Alec."

Shannon sighed. She didn't want the brief moment of respite to end, but Kate was right. No sense in putting off either task. "Thank you. I'll go to the office to make my call, and I'll ask Essie to bring out cleaning supplies."

Reluctantly, she stood and headed down the aisle. By her calculations, Alec should have finished dinner. She hoped she could catch him before he sat down to study. She found Essie at the back door, scrubbing up black powder.

Essie looked up. "Finished with your group already?"

"We decided to forgo knitting and start cleaning, and I have a call to make. Can you round up more cleaning supplies and take them out to the group?"

"Sure." Essie smiled. "It's great you have such good friends to help out with this."

"It is indeed," Shannon said as she walked into her office.

The small space held traces of fingerprint powder like the rest of the shop, but not nearly as much. She grabbed a tissue to wipe off the arms of her grandmother's antique wooden chair, then sat on the needlepoint cushion.

Her cellphone chimed Lara's ringtone. Fearful that her daughter was calling to report more bad news, Shannon hurried to answer and nearly dropped the phone in her haste. "Lara, is everything OK?"

"Gosh, Mum." Lara sounded exasperated. "Why are you so freaked out?"

Because I'm a mother, and my child is having a hard time, she thought. But Lara would never understand until she had her own children. "Alec never called me back, so I thought you might be calling to give me bad news."

"Um, no. I called to see if you'd talked to him, but I guess you didn't." There was a gentle softness in her voice as she talked about Alec—a softness she reserved exclusively for her twin.

"I left him a message." Shannon stifled a sigh that was desperate to escape. "Have you seen him since we talked?"

"An hour ago at the library. He was supposed to be studying, but all he did was stare off into space." Lara paused, and Shannon heard her call-waiting beep.

"Hold on a sec," Shannon said. "I have a call coming in, maybe it's Alec." She glanced at the phone and saw her mother's name and number on the screen. Disappointed, she let Beth's call roll to voice mail and returned her attention to Lara.

"It wasn't Alec." Shannon didn't elaborate on who it was; as she hadn't yet come to grips with having her mother in her life again. She didn't plan to tell her children any more about Beth until she'd decided how she and Beth would move forward after thirty-six years without any contact.

"So anyway," Lara continued, "I asked Alec if something was wrong, but he snapped at me to mind my own business. That's why I wanted to know if you'd talked to him."

Shannon released her pent-up sigh. This was not like Alec at all. He was usually kind and considerate—cooperative, not moody. "I wonder what's gotten into him."

"I don't know," Lara said, "but it's really odd."

"I can phone him again," Shannon offered absently, trying to think of how she could help from thousands of miles away. "Or maybe I could call Coleen, and she could drive down to check on him."

"Oh, Mum, no! Do *not* send Coleen. That would only embarrass him and make him clam up more."

Shannon wasn't sure Lara was right about that. Coleen had a way with Alec; she always had. She could get him to open up about most anything. Still, Shannon wouldn't take that step before talking with him at least. "I'll give him another call."

"And you won't dispatch Coleen over here?"

"Not yet."

Lara blew out a breath. "Good. Let me know the minute you talk to him."

Shannon disconnected and dialed Alec. The phone rang until his voice mail message played. "Alec, it's me again," she said. "Please call me *today*. No matter what time you get this message, I need to talk to you."

Feeling dejected, she hung up and pressed the screen to bring up her own voice mail. As she waited for the message to queue up, she clutched the locket she'd worn on a silver chain since the day she'd received it from her grandmother's attorney. Inside was a picture of her own mother, Beth, as a little girl.

The message played, and she heard Beth clear her throat before speaking. "Just following up to see if you have time for that lunch we talked about," Beth said. "I think we should get together and talk, don't you? I'd love to see you. Call me."

Shannon deleted the message and looked at the shelves filled with her grandmother's crafts that spoke of her family's history. Shannon had missed out on so much. Perhaps she was still missing out by not making more of an effort to connect with her mother, now that she finally had the chance.

But dealing with Alec's problem and a murder mystery was all she could handle right now. Figuring things out with her mother would have to wait.

*   *   *

Shannon drew the blinds closed in her craft room, and the wooden slats clacked into place. Night had descended as she and Melanie scoured Edward's files for clues. Hours poring over records copied at his apartment had left Shannon feeling unsettled, and she couldn't shake the notion that someone was watching them through the darkened window. She patted the slats, pressing a few stubborn ones closed.

With unease curdling the hasty meal they had consumed, Shannon returned to her desk and sat down. She wanted to suggest they knock off for the night, but she needed to help Melanie more than she needed sleep.

Melanie yawned as she looked up from the side chair where she had been organizing a new batch of pages. "Seems to me we're missing the key item here."

"What's that?" Shannon asked as she neatly stacked the pages they'd already reviewed.

"Grayson said Angie's jealous boyfriend has been texting Ed. If we had access to Ed's phone records, we could find the number of the man texting him."

Shannon felt a pinch of anticipation at the idea. She found the same excitement in Melanie's eyes. "Do you know the company Edward used for his cellphone?"

"If he didn't change carriers, I do. Why?"

"I can access my account online," Shannon said, opening her laptop. "My user name is my phone number, and Edward could have the same type of login. If we could come up with a password he might have used, we can access his account."

"It's worth a try." Melanie inched closer to the computer. "Thank goodness Ed didn't like change. He's had the same number for the last fifteen years, and I know he kept it when we split up." Melanie rattled off the carrier and Edward's phone number.

Shannon entered the number on the carrier's website. "Now ... any ideas about his password?"

"That one should be easy. No matter how many times I told him not to, he always used a combination of his name and birth date." Melanie grabbed a notepad and jotted down some characters.

Shannon typed them into the password box, and the computer churned away. It idled for so long, she began to fear they'd been wrong—but then the account opened.

"It worked!" Shannon exclaimed.

"I *told* him it wasn't safe to use such a simple password," Melanie grumbled. "For once I'm glad the man never listened to me."

Shannon read the options on the screen, then opened the section with his most recent calls and ran down the list. "Look at this one." She pointed to a number on the screen. "Seems like a frequent caller."

"Check the text log."

Shannon changed pages to see the summary of his text calls. "Frequent flyer here too."

Melanie frowned. "So we have the number. How's that going to help us?"

"We use a reverse phone number lookup site to get the address it's associated with." Shannon started typing in a search box.

"And how do you know about such a site?" Melanie asked.

"Someone was sending Lara spam texts and using up all of her allotted texts for the month. She wanted me to change our plan to unlimited texts, but I couldn't afford it, so she and Alec tracked down the spammer this way."

Melanie laughed. "Never thought I'd be thankful for spam."

Shannon opened a new tab and searched for a reverse phone lookup site. The computer churned again. A handful of choices popped up on the screen. Shannon perused the top three and clicked one.

"This one ought to work," she said. She entered the phone number and waited as the program searched the phone database. After a few seconds, the word "Unlisted" flashed on the screen. Deflated, Shannon sat back. "Ugh! I'd really hoped this would lead somewhere."

"Me too." Melanie's shoulders slumped. "Maybe we could get the ex's information from Angie."

"Edward's girlfriend? Do you honestly think she'd tell us about her ex?"

Melanie paused, seeming to consider the question. "If she thinks he killed Ed, then yes, I think she would. Greg said she's employed at Salty's Seafood. We could call them to see when she usually works and then pay her a visit."

"Great idea." Shannon quickly searched for the restaurant's phone number, then grabbed her cellphone and dialed. A woman answered on the first ring.

"Salty's Seafood. The freshest catch in Portland." The greeting competed with clanking dishes in the background.

"Is Angie Carson working tonight?" Shannon asked loudly.

"She only works the day shift."

"So she'll be there tomorrow?"

"Probably," the disinterested female responded.

"OK, thanks." Shannon hung up, looked at Melanie, then smiled. "I have a sudden craving for seafood. How about lunch at Salty's tomorrow?"

"It's a plan."

— 9 —

At the craft store the next morning, Shannon hummed as she filled a clear plastic bin with a new angora yarn that she'd been dying to use. The baby-soft yarn felt wonderful against her fingers. It also felt wonderful to be engaged in a routine activity that carried no earth-shattering consequences if she made a mistake. She'd barely slept the previous two nights, thinking about how Grayson was set on blaming Melanie for the murder. That, mixed with worry about Alec, meant another night of tossing and turning in her usually tranquil bedroom.

But she was done worrying. Today was a fresh day— a perfect day to talk to Alec and help him resolve whatever issue he was facing.

"One that holds promise for better things," Shannon mumbled as she broke down a cardboard box.

"What's that?" Essie asked from a far corner of the shop, where she was busy ordering supplies.

Shannon waved her hand in the air. "Sorry. Talking to myself again."

Essie responded with a raised brow. "Other than a few strange mutterings to yourself, you've been very quiet this morning. Is there anything I can help you with?"

What a sweetheart—and such a good worker. Shannon felt a brief urge to share with Essie about her recent struggles. But she didn't want to do anything to risk ruining their working relationship so she shook her head.

"No, but thanks for the offer." Shannon picked up a stack of empty boxes. "I'm going to dispose of these, then do some paperwork. Send Melanie back when she arrives, OK?"

"You got it," Essie said cheerfully. At least she didn't seem hurt by Shannon's lack of sharing.

Shannon put the boxes in a recycle pile and hurried to her office. Her grandmother's nameplate rattled as she opened the door. She lowered herself into the softly cushioned chair behind the desk where her connection to her grandmother always felt the strongest. She could almost picture her grandmother sitting in the very same chair, working on crafts or bookwork for the shop.

Shannon eyed the mound of waiting paperwork, then she picked up her phone and dialed her son.

"Mum." He answered on the second ring, his one-word greeting dripping with irritation.

"Alec, I'm glad I finally got you instead of your voice mail." She tried not to sound hurt by his failure to return any of her calls; she knew that would only put him on the defensive.

"What do you want?"

Och, he was just as cranky as Lara had said. "I hadn't heard from you in a while, and I wanted to check in."

"I've been busy."

Shannon didn't believe him for one minute. "Busy with what?"

"Studying. With the semester ending, I have my plate full, you know."

"How are your classes going?" she asked, knowing his classes were something he loved to discuss and should be a safe topic.

"Fine."

So much for the discussion. "Is something troubling you, Alec?"

"No."

She refused to let him put her off. "You're usually a lot more talkative than this, so it seems to me something's up."

He sighed and the heavy breath filled the phone. "You worry too much. I'm sorry, but I have to go."

She didn't want to hang up, but she also didn't want to antagonize him when something was obviously troubling him. "OK, call me when you have more time. I love you."

"Love you too." He hung up, and Shannon sat back in her chair.

She'd had similar conversations with Alec early on in his high school years. He was a teenager, after all, and he had things he needed to work through. But he'd outgrown the angst as he'd matured. Something about his current tone worried her more. Perhaps it was simply the fact that he was thousands of miles away, and she couldn't see his face to determine how badly he was feeling.

Without another thought, she dialed her friend, Coleen, in Scotland.

"Hello," Coleen answered.

At the sound of her dearest friend's voice, tears formed in Shannon's eyes. "I'm so glad you're home."

"Oh, land sakes, but it's good to hear your voice, girl!"

Hearing Coleen's rich accent barreling through the

phone felt like a homecoming. "I've missed you too," Shannon eked out.

"Is that loneliness I'm hearing?" Coleen asked, her concern spilling over and easing Shannon's pain.

"Yes, and a good measure of worry too." She filled Coleen in on everything that had been happening with Alec.

"The boy has a good head on his shoulders," Coleen said. "You raised him right, and he'll be fine."

"I hope you're right."

After a long pause, Coleen said, "You want me to go check on him, don't you?"

"Would you?"

Another pause, this one even longer, followed. "Do you really think that's such a good idea?"

"Yes ... no ... I don't know. But it's what I want you to do," Shannon said. "That is, if you can do it without letting on that I asked you to go. Make it appear like you just happened to be in town and wanted to take him out for a meal."

"Now don't you worry. Subtlety is my forté." Coleen laughed at the absurdity of her own statement.

"Right." Shannon laughed heartily with her friend. For a brief moment, she had second thoughts about the plan. But she knew she had to do *something*. She pushed her concerns out of her mind, and settled in for a long conversation. She shared all that had happened in Apple Grove since they had spoken last. Coleen asked Shannon to give Melanie an encouraging hug and say hello to all of the Purls for her. As usual, once they'd finished talking, Shannon felt lighter, and she was eager to get to work.

She pulled out invoices that needed review and payment

from a basket on the desk. Working diligently through the stack, she hummed to herself until she recaptured the positive mood with which she'd started the day.

"Ready for lunch?" Melanie asked, poking her head in the office.

At her friend's cheerful tone, Shannon looked up. She noted that Melanie's outfit didn't include a jacket.

"Yes. Sun's out, I take it?" Shannon asked as she got up and grabbed her purse off a hook by the door.

"It's a beautiful day," Melanie said. "Makes me wish we didn't have to be cooped up in a car and we could take a nice long walk instead."

Shannon slipped her arm around Melanie. "You seem like you got a good night's sleep last night," she said.

Melanie nodded. "I did. Wish I could say the same thing to you."

Shannon removed her arm and cast a mock look of horror at her friend. "I don't look *that* tired, do I?"

"In all seriousness," Melanie said as they walked through the shop, "I hope this thing with Ed isn't keeping you up."

"I'm afraid it is. That and Alec, actually." Shannon paused in the paper section, where Essie was busy filling an empty bin with colorful handcrafted paper. "Can you close up for me if I don't make it back in time?" Shannon asked.

"Sure," Essie said. "You two have a nice lunch."

Shannon opened the door for Melanie, and they walked outside, into the warmth of the sun. As usual for the time of year, the earlier overcast skies had burned off, and it promised to be one of those glorious days they'd longed for during the rainy winter season.

They climbed into Melanie's small SUV and set off for Portland. Melanie snapped on the radio, and jazz music filled the car.

Shannon stared out the passenger window, watching the businesses of Apple Grove pass by. How she loved the little town—the charming shops, the friendly people, the good friends she'd made in the Purls. Apple Grove felt like home in so many ways, and it would feel even more so once the twins arrived.

"You want to talk about Alec?" Melanie asked.

"I don't know ... maybe." Shannon swiveled in the seat to face her friend. "You've raised an amazing son. How did you get through the young adult years?"

"Lots of prayer and biting my tongue," Melanie said as she clicked on her blinker before turning onto the highway.

"I'm serious, Mel."

"Me too. When Greg first went off to college, I tried to stay just as involved in his life as if he were still living at home. But he let me know loud and clear he wouldn't put up with that much interference."

"Do you think that's what Alec's doing?"

"Could be, but it sounds more like he's trying to work through something, and he wants space to do it."

"I understand that part, but what I don't know is how to give him the space he needs," Shannon said. "Not when I'm so worried about him."

"I get it. Believe me, I get it." Melanie stepped on the gas as they started to climb the first hill that led into the Coast Range populated with thick forests of tall pines. "I finally decided with Greg that whenever I wanted to interfere, I'd ask myself what was the worst thing that could happen if I let him make the mistake he seemed headed for. If it wasn't anything that could ruin his life or get him killed, I backed off. After a while, he started coming to me with the big decisions."

Shannon processed the advice. "It sounds like a good plan, but I don't even know what's bothering Alec. It *could* be life-threatening for all I know."

"From everything I've seen and heard about you two, I can't imagine he wouldn't come to you if it was something that serious." Melanie glanced at her friend. "Or at the very least, if he does have a serious problem, he'd tell Lara, right?"

"You're right, he would." Shannon felt the heavy weight lifting from her shoulders. "I wish I'd talked to you before I made a mess of things by nagging him into talking to me."

"Don't worry—it's not that big of a mess. At least not one you can't recover from."

"I wish children came with some sort of 'how-to' manual, you know? It'd make raising them a whole lot simpler."

Melanie laughed. "That book would be so thick, you'd never be able to lift it."

"I guess I always assumed it would get easier when they grew up."

Melanie shook her head. "You may stop *raising* a child, but you never stop worrying about them."

The radio announced upcoming news, and Melanie turned it up. "I'd like to listen in case they say anything about Ed."

Shannon sat back and let her mind drift. She wished—

as she had wished many times while raising Alec and Lara—that she could go to her own mother for advice. Back then, it was a useless wish because she didn't know where her mother was. But now? Now she needed to come to grips with the residual hurt she felt from being abandoned as a child—even if her mother had a good reason for doing what she did.

Her hand drifted to her locket again. When a commercial came on, Shannon glanced at Melanie. "Do you think I'm being too hard on my mother?"

Melanie flashed a surprised look. "You mean by not letting her into your life without taking some time to think about it first?"

"Yes."

"Where's that coming from all of a sudden?"

"She called and wants to have lunch, but I've been putting her off. It's crazy, I've dreamed of having a mother my whole life, and now that I know where she is, you'd think I'd jump at the chance to spend endless hours with her."

Melanie gave her a reassuring smile. "You will. Give it time."

"In other news," the announcer said, "a source close to the Edward Burkhart murder investigation in Apple Grove tells us his former wife, Melanie Burkhart, is the prime suspect in the case."

Melanie gasped and jerked the wheel.

"Och!" Shannon exclaimed, clinging to the dashboard.

"Sorry."

When the SUV stopped swaying, Shannon let go with one hand and turned up the volume.

The announcer's voice blared from the speakers. "Apple Grove Police Chief Jack Grayson refused to confirm the allegations that Mrs. Burkhart doesn't have an alibi for the time of death. He says they're working every lead and will keep us informed of any breaking developments."

"I need to call Greg," Melanie said, sounding panicked. "If he hears this, he'll flip out."

"Pull over at the next turnout, and I'll drive so you can call."

Melanie nodded, then retreated behind worried eyes. How quickly things could change.

* * *

Lunch business at Salty's Seafood was slow. Shannon requested they be seated in Angie's section, and the hostess accommodated them with a disinterested shrug.

Angie emerged from the kitchen, and Shannon watched her wind gracefully among the tables toward them. She wore jeans and a navy T-shirt boasting a large anchor with "Salty's Seafood" scrawled across it. She was model tall and thin, and she wore her makeup caked on. Her bottle-blond hair fell in thick waves to her shoulders.

"She's pretty isn't she?" Melanie asked, a hint of jealousy in her voice.

"In a fake, brittle sort of way, I suppose she is."

Melanie snorted. "A classic friend's answer to discovering your ex's new girlfriend is drop-dead gorgeous."

"Ladies," Angie said when she stopped at their table. Her long lashes rested on her cheeks every time she blinked, drawing attention to the dark circles below her eyes. "What can I get you to drink?"

"Iced tea," Shannon said.

"The same." Melanie couldn't seem to take her gaze off Angie.

Angie raised one perfectly plucked brow. "Do I know you?"

"I'm Melanie, Ed's former wife," Melanie blurted.

A look of shock flashed on Angie's face and she dropped into a chair as if her legs could no longer support her. "Are you here to talk about Ed?"

"Yes."

Tears formed in Angie's startling blue eyes. "I still can't believe he's gone."

"I know. Do you have any idea who might've wanted him dead?" Melanie asked. Her mild-mannered personality had disappeared behind a tough veneer.

Angie stared at Melanie. "The police think *you* did."

Melanie pulled back her shoulders, but didn't look away. "Do you share their opinion?"

Angie glanced at the door for a few moments, as if debating whether or not to run away. Then her eyes darted back to Melanie. "I'd be royally miffed if Ed bailed on me the way he bailed on you. But no, I can tell from the amazing son you raised that you aren't capable of murder."

"Thanks," Melanie said, her demeanor visibly softening. "So who do you think did it?"

"I have an ex-boyfriend, Buddy." Angie's expression was tight. "He has a bad temper. That's why we split up. He didn't like that I left him, and he turned real ugly when he found out Ed and I were an item. I don't know if he's capable of killing anyone, but when he's been drinking, he's pretty mean."

"Did you know he was sending threatening texts to Edward?" Shannon asked.

Angie turned to Shannon, eyeing her suspiciously. "And you are?"

"I'm Shannon McClain." Shannon smiled to ease the woman's obvious concern. "I live in Apple Grove too. Melanie asked me to help her find out who killed Edward."

Angie's gaze shifted to Melanie.

"It's OK," Melanie said.

Angie shrugged. "I knew about the texts. But Ed didn't seem worried. Now I'm thinking maybe he should've been."

"Could you give us this boyfriend's full name, address and phone number?" Shannon pressed.

"I can." Angie glanced at Melanie, then back at Shannon, warning them with her look. "But trust me—the two of you don't want to go see him alone."

"That bad, huh?" Melanie asked.

"Only when he's been drinking. And from what I've heard, he's been doing a lot of that since I left."

"We'll be careful, then." Melanie dug out a notepad and pen from her purse. "Can you write down the information we need?"

Angie scribbled the information and slid the pad back at Melanie. "He works nights, so the best time of day to catch him home and sober is late morning."

Shannon could hardly contain her excitement about finally having a firm lead to work with. "By chance, do you know anything about Edward's most recent employer?"

"Sure," Angie said. "He worked for Portland Aviation, but he never talked much about them."

Shannon felt another wave of adrenaline crash over her as they learned the name of Edward's employer. "Did he ever complain about the job?" she asked. "Or did he have issues with his salary or problems with his boss?"

"Nah, he made good money. He always had money to burn, and he didn't have to work long hours, like I do here, so he never complained." Angie looked around. "This place barely pays my rent. With Ed gone, I'll never get to do anything fun again." She wiped the back of her hand across eyes filling with fresh tears and abruptly stood. "Do you still want to have lunch, or are you in a hurry to get out of here?"

Shannon actually felt sorry for Angie. Melanie's kind-hearted expression said she did too. "We're here to eat. What do you recommend?"

"Our clam chowder is the best in Oregon. We serve it in a bread bowl with Salty's famous coleslaw on the side."

"Then I'll have the clam chowder," Melanie said, handing Angie her menu.

"Same for me," Shannon said.

When Angie had moved out of earshot, Melanie said, "Are you thinking what I'm thinking?"

Shannon nodded. "We need to pay Buddy a visit."

She heard the anticipation in her own voice. She wanted to race out of the restaurant and track the guy down that very moment. But first they needed to devise a plan to get him to talk. Something told her that showing up at his front door, and politely asking if he'd killed anyone lately probably wouldn't end well.

— 10 —

At home in the study, Shannon stared at her hands, illuminated by the blue hue of her computer screen, and stifled a yawn. For the last four hours, she'd looked up the various websites Edward had visited before his death. She should have been much farther down the list, but she'd been distracted by thoughts about her earlier decision not to race over to Buddy's place. Now she was wondering if she and Melanie had made the wrong decision.

As they'd sat at Salty's Seafood, devouring chowder thick with clams and rich, creamy broth, they'd discussed a plan to visit Buddy. They felt certain Angie wouldn't have warned them not to go alone if she didn't have a good reason. It wasn't safe—pure and simple, not safe. So despite their excitement about the lead, they'd decided to wait until they could find someone to accompany them.

In the meantime, Shannon would look into other aspects of Edward's life—aspects like Edward's excess cash. From the way Angie talked about his free spending, Melanie felt certain he'd been supplementing his income. Maybe he was doing something illegal? Thus far, Shannon had only learned that a man named Paul Wilson owned Portland Aviation.

She focused on her task, running her finger down the browser list she'd printed off Edward's computer. Her finger stilled above the link for the next site she needed to visit.

From the Web address, she could tell the link was generated by search results for helicopters and pollution. She navigated to the site, but nothing obvious jumped out, so she followed Edward's browsing trail deeper. He'd viewed multiple helicopter maintenance requirements on the Federal Aviation Administration's website and various Oregon coastal pollution sites.

Perhaps Edward caught his employer polluting the ocean and blackmailed him? Or maybe the pollution and maintenance pages weren't related to the case at all. Either way, if he was blackmailing his boss for doing something illegal, the boss might have grown tired of paying Edward and ended it by killing him and framing Melanie.

Shannon felt a familiar hint of excitement bubbling up again. Despite the late hour, she grabbed her phone and dialed Melanie.

"Mel," she said the second her friend answered, "has Greg gotten back to you about Edward's bank accounts yet?"

"No." Melanie didn't sound the least bit tired. "Do you want me to call him?"

Shannon filled her in on the FAA discovery. "This doesn't mean Edward was blackmailing his boss, but it's possible."

"If we find an unusually large sum of money or frequent cash deposits in his account, it could be likely though, right?" Melanie asked.

"Right."

"I'll call Greg as soon as we hang up." Melanie's eagerness carried through the phone. "With any luck, he'll answer and I can call you right back."

"Great. Either way, I've decided I'm going to Portland Aviation to visit with Edward's boss tomorrow."

"Oh, I wish I could go with you, but I have to work," Melanie said with a sigh. "Of all the days for Elaina to go out of town."

"I wish you could come with me too. But I think we should try to resolve this as soon as possible." Shannon felt certain they needed to find something to clear Melanie's name soon—before Grayson arrested her.

"I agree, but I would feel better about you going without me if you borrowed my SUV," Melanie said. "I'd worry that your old truck wouldn't make it to Portland and back."

Shannon had had the same thought, and she appreciated her friend's considerate gesture. "Thanks, I'll take you up on the offer."

"And we need to get Kate's pepper spray too—that small can she clips on her key ring when she walks dogs late at night," Melanie suggested.

"I'll think about the pepper spray, OK?"

"I don't want anything to happen to you."

"I know, and I appreciate your concern. If you don't call me back about Greg tonight, I'll stop by The Flower Pot in the morning to see if you've heard from him."

Shannon hung up and shut down her computer. She waited until the computer fan quit whirring to close the case.

Suddenly a strange noise sounded at the front door, and Shannon swiveled in her chair to listen. Footfalls thumped on the porch, then hurried down the stairs.

Who would be at the door at this hour?

Her pulse beat double-time. She scanned the room for a makeshift weapon and saw a thick wooden dowel leaning against the wall in the corner. She hopped up and grabbed it.

Clutching the piece of wood like a baseball bat, she held it over her shoulder, ready to swing if she encountered a problem.

Stepping into the dimly lit hallway, she searched through the darkness. Moonlight filtered through the window in the door, casting shadows in every corner of the entryway.

Oh, how I wish Deborah wasn't out of town right now!

A shiver started at Shannon's head and worked its way down her body as she crept toward the light switch.

A car engine cranked in the distance, halting her steps. She heard the engine catch and roar, tires squealing as the vehicle spun on the pavement and grabbed hold.

Frozen in place, she listened, waiting ... as the dark closed in on her. She wanted to flip on every light within reach, but then she'd be visible to anyone lurking outside. She heard the car engine purr for a moment, and then the sound grew faint as it sped away.

Shannon relaxed a notch and slowed her breathing so she could think clearly. The car was too far away to be related to the footfalls she'd heard.

Or was it?

If someone had indeed run down her steps, they'd have had time to race to the road and take off while she searched for a weapon and made her way through the darkened foyer.

She debated calling the police. *But what will I tell them—that I thought I heard a car driving on the road? Not exactly a crime.*

No, she needed something concrete if she was going to call the police. Leaving the light off, she edged toward the door. Gripping the dowel tightly, she skirted around the marble table and inched forward.

Once at the door, she braved a quick glance out the window before flattening her back against the wall. She saw nothing unusual, but she counted to ten before looking again.

She flipped on the porch light and took another brief look, this one a little longer. Still nothing. She held her breath, thinking it might help her detect the faintest noise of movement outside. Save for her heart thundering in her chest and crickets chirping outside, she heard nothing.

Feeling a little foolish, she peeled herself away from the wall. After days on end filled with talk of murder, her imagination was clearly running wild.

"I'm losing my mind," she muttered as she unlocked the door so she could check the porch thoroughly for her own peace of mind. She stepped onto the porch and froze.

A large manila envelope lay tucked under the edge of the tulip welcome mat.

Someone *had* been on her porch.

Shannon grabbed the envelope, then darted back into the house. She slammed the door shut and twisted the deadbolt as far as it would go.

Once safely inside, she studied the envelope, blank and sealed tight. A sense of foreboding washed over her as she recalled the last time she'd found an anonymous letter on her front porch—in Scotland. The discovery had marked the beginning of a very dangerous journey.

An owl hooted in the distance, and she jumped. *Standing in front of the window probably isn't the smartest idea.* Shannon hurried through the foyer and took refuge in her study. She closed and locked that door as well, then sat down to open the envelope before her legs collapsed from stress.

With trembling fingers, she tore open the envelope and peered inside. It contained one item—a newspaper article about the dedication ceremony, including a photograph of Shannon. The headline read "Murder by Knitting Needle." Someone had circled her head with a thick red marker and scratched a big X over her face.

They'd written a message below it.

"BACK OFF, OR THE OTHER NEEDLE WILL BE FOR YOU!"

Gasping, Shannon released the paper. It floated to the floor and slid beneath a chair. She grabbed her phone, and with a trembling finger, she dialed Grayson's direct number. The phone rang five times before he answered.

"You'd better have a good reason for calling me at home at this hour," he grumbled, sounding sleepy.

"It's Shannon McClain. Someone left a threatening note on my porch," she blurted.

"When?"

"Just now."

"Where are you?"

"In my study with the door locked."

"Stay put," he said. "I'm on my way."

Shannon disconnected but held her phone at the ready and watched the door. She suspected that whoever had left the message had completed their mission and wouldn't be back anytime soon. Even so, she remained holed up in the study until Grayson pounded loudly on the front door and announced himself.

Shannon retrieved the newspaper clipping from under the chair and grabbed the envelope before going to the front door. She opened it to find Grayson pacing the length of the front porch. He wore jeans and a navy windbreaker with an Apple Grove Police Department logo on the chest.

"Thanks for coming." Shannon held out the envelope and article.

Gently, Grayson lifted them at the edges and turned them over. She felt a bit guilty for treating them so carelessly, but she'd been in shock.

"Where did you say you found this?" he asked.

"Under the doormat."

"Did you see who left it?"

"No," she said. "I heard someone running down the steps, then a little while later, a car started at the road."

Grayson carefully put the clipping back in the envelope and took it to his car. As he walked back toward the porch, he bent to check something in the garden bed next to the walkway. "Here's a fresh footprint in the dirt," he said, pulling a small flashlight from his pocket. "From the size, it looks like a male athletic shoe. I might be able to cast a footprint, but it looks like a common tread so it's not likely to give us a good lead."

"What about prints on the newspaper and envelope?"

"We'll process them," Grayson said, his expression grim, "but even if we do lift a good print, that doesn't mean we'll find a matching set in the database. I suggest you heed the warning and leave the investigating to professionals."

She swallowed hard. "Do you really think someone might try to kill me?"

"Unfortunately, that's not the kind of thing I can predict. But it'd sure make my job a lot easier if I could."

Shannon felt a chill run through her and wished she
could back off. But that wasn't an option. She'd promised
Melanie she would help her. And making sure Melanie didn't
go to jail for a crime she didn't commit was far too important.

*   *   *

Shannon held her hand over her eyes to block the
morning sun and watched as the construction workers
build wooden forms in preparation for pouring the concrete
foundation of Espresso Yourself. They'd resumed construction
at sunup that morning, and Shannon was impressed with
their quick progress.

She turned to the construction supervisor. "Do you
honestly think you can get back on schedule?" she asked,
raising her voice to be heard above the pounding hammers
and buzzing saws.

"Yeah, sure. *If* the weather holds." He shifted his hard
hat and scratched his forehead. "But that's a big if during
this time of year."

"You'll keep me updated on any delays?"

"You betcha." He stuck out his hand, signaling the end
of the progress report.

Shannon took hold of his calloused fingers and shook.
Then he went back to the job, and she rushed through the alley
to the back door of the shop. Even in her office, construction
noise rattled the window. But since it was the sound of her
addition under way once again, it was music to her ears.

Ready to leave for her visit to Portland Aviation, she
grabbed her purse and headed down the main aisle of the

shop. She spotted Essie, in her bright, tie-dyed skirt and long turquoise tunic, telling a customer goodbye. The morning newspaper lay on the countertop, reminding Shannon of the previous night's cryptic warning. The fear she'd felt still lingered, and it made her uneasy, but she was determined not to let it detour her.

"Looks like your customer bought half the store," Shannon said to Essie, eyeing the large brown bag the customer carried out the door.

"It's all yarn for baby afghans." Essie's face held a faint look of amusement. "She has three grandchildren on the way."

"My goodness."

"My thoughts exactly." Essie closed the cash register drawer with a firm clunk. "You on your way out?"

"Yes, and I'm so sorry to leave you alone again today. I wouldn't do this to you if it wasn't important."

"No biggie. As long as we have a few minutes, like we did this morning, to catch up and work through any problems, I'm good."

"Thank you for being so responsible," Shannon said. "I should be back late this afternoon, and you can go home early for once."

"That would be nice. I'd like to get the beading work done on the latest pendants you made." Essie slipped a wayward tendril of her blond hair behind one ear. "The silver is stunning, by the way. You did an amazing job on them."

Shannon smiled her appreciation. Essie had proven herself to be a very talented beader, and she'd been enthusiastic about Shannon's new hobby, silversmithing jewelry, from day one. Still in her 20s, Essie's youthful eye kept their designs fresh and appealing to the young tourist market. Together they made a great design team.

"The jewelry would be nothing without your beading. You caught on so fast, and you surpassed anything I've ever done," Shannon said.

Essie laughed. "Listen to us. We sound like a couple of brownnosers." She wrinkled her nose. It was clear the straightforward Essie would rather die than be accused of anything like brownnosing.

"Or it's more like we have a mutual respect for something we both love," Shannon countered.

Essie nodded her approval. "I like the sound of that better. Have a safe trip."

"Thanks." Shannon waved, then stepped outside.

The scent of fresh baked goods from Pink Sprinkles Bakery rode the ocean breeze down the street and sent her stomach growling for one of Joyce's signature apple fritters. But she ignored the late morning grumble and dug Melanie's keys from her purse, thankful for her friend's offer to loan her the SUV for the drive to Portland. Rumbling and bouncing all the way to the city in her grandma's old truck would not be nearly as enjoyable. The sight of the pepper spray dangling from Melanie's key ring made her chuckle. Melanie had picked it up from Kate at Ultimutt Grooming on her way to work. By the time Shannon had stopped by The Flower Pot to see Melanie, it was ready and waiting for her. Unfortunately, the news from Greg hadn't been good. He'd been too busy at work to find time to track down Edward's finances.

Shannon climbed into Melanie's SUV and slid the seat forward to accommodate her shorter legs. She plugged

Portland Aviation's address into the GPS and followed the directions from the robotic voice, missing only one turn and having to backtrack before parking in a lot that overlooked the airfield. Several small planes and helicopters sat outside the small hangar. She made her way to the main entrance, smoothing her khaki pants and knit top before stepping over the threshold.

The lushly appointed reception area held contemporary chocolate furniture, glass tables, and large plants grouped in an intimate seating area at one end and a mahogany reception desk at the other. If the chic lobby was any indication, business was thriving.

Shannon headed straight for the receptionist, who looked to be fresh out of high school. The way she mashed on her pink wad of gum made Shannon wonder if she was even that old. The name "Bethany" was engraved on a small plaque behind a neat row of business card holders.

"I'm here to see Paul," Shannon said.

"You have an appointment?" Bethany lifted her hand to examine the purple polish on her fingernails.

"No, but I'd like to talk to someone about a tour. I understand Paul owns the company, and I thought I'd start at the top."

Bethany shrugged and picked up her phone, and within five minutes, Shannon was seated in Paul Wilson's office. He was a tall man, in his 40s, Shannon guessed, dressed in a navy suit and very professional in his manner—truly the opposite of Bethany. He hardly seemed the type to be doing anything illegal. Not that Shannon had any idea if there was a "type" for that.

"You want to talk about a tour?" he asked.

Shannon had worked hard to concoct a cover story, but as nerves set in, she worried that she wouldn't be convincing. It would be difficult to question him without resorting to lying. "I'm a nervous flyer," she said. "I wondered if we could talk about safety."

"Of course. We have only the most qualified pilots and adhere to stringent safety standards." If her chosen topic bothered Paul, his relaxed posture didn't show it.

"Good to know. I was also wondering if you're required to follow rules set forth by the FAA."

"Absolutely. We meet or exceed all of their regulations and maintain our aircraft accordingly."

Shannon smiled. "That's great. And you've never had any issues with violations?"

"None." He returned her smile, and it seemed earnest enough. "It's refreshing to see someone interested in safety instead of blindly trusting any old helicopter company. How did you hear about us, anyway?"

Time to take off the gloves. "Edward Burkhart."

"Ah … Ed. Poor guy." Paul sounded sincere, but his eyes narrowed slightly.

Shannon gave an acknowledging nod. "It was a shock, for sure. I can't imagine who would do such a thing to him— can you?"

Paul briefly glanced to the right, a behavior Shannon had learned from her favorite forensic show might mean he was about to lie to her. "No," he said firmly.

"You don't think his death could have anything to do with his job, do you?" she asked. "I mean, maybe someone here didn't like him?"

"He was an upstanding guy and a good worker. Everyone around here liked him. I—" Paul's voice trailed off as if he was unsure he should continue.

"Did *you* get along with him?" Shannon pressed.

Paul watched her for a long, uncomfortable moment before he spoke, "Are you here to arrange a tour or to accuse me of killing Ed?"

"Should I have reason to accuse you?" For a second she felt like Michael, always answering a question with a question.

"If you don't want to talk about a tour then our conversation is over." He moved abruptly to stand, pushing back with such force that his trendy desk chair crashed into the wall.

Shannon felt sure that a man with nothing to hide would declare his innocence instead of ending the conversation. *He must be hiding something.*

Shannon stood. "I can see myself out."

She breezed into the lobby, and after looking back to make sure Paul hadn't followed, she zipped over to the reception desk.

Shannon smiled at Bethany. "Quick question, did you know Edward Burkhart?"

"Ed ... yeah, sure."

"Paul says everyone around here liked him. Would you agree?"

Bethany thought for a moment. "If that's what Paul said, it must be true."

"But what do *you* think?" Shannon asked, trying not to show her impatience.

Bethany glanced past Shannon, then slid closer. "Between

you and me, something weird was going on between Paul and Ed. I caught them whispering about something a few times. They always stopped talking when they saw me."

"Did Paul seem angry?"

"Angry?" She looked down. Her long lashes, coated with thick mascara, batted as rapidly as a hummingbird's wings. "No. He acted like they were talking about something they didn't want anyone else to know about."

"Have you heard any rumors about him or the business having problems?" Shannon asked.

"No." Bethany suddenly turned away and started shuffling papers. "Look, Paul's heading over here, and he doesn't look happy. You should go. I can't get involved in anything that will get me fired."

"Thanks for the directions," Shannon announced loud enough for Paul to hear so he wouldn't get mad at Bethany.

She backed away from the desk and nodded at Paul. She could feel his eyes following her as she exited the building and walked to the car.

What are you hiding, Paul Wilson?

— **11** —

Shannon placed a tea tray on the glass counter next to the plate of peanut butter cookies she'd baked in the wee hours of the night when the dire newspaper warning had kept her awake. Then she pulled up a stool and sat across the counter from Michael. After Essie had departed for the day, Shannon had phoned him to ask if he could think of any illegal activities Paul Wilson might be involved in. Michael said he could come up with a few ideas, but he insisted on stopping by the store to discuss them with her in person.

"Do you take anything in your tea?" she asked as she poured the rich Darjeeling blend into a cup.

"I'm not sure." He stared at the tea like it was poison. "I'm not really a tea drinker."

Her head snapped up. "You should've said something. I could have made coffee."

"I figured it was a chance to try something new." He smiled, easing some of her discomfort. "Why don't you serve mine the same way you drink yours?"

She poured milk into his cup, then added a scoop of sugar. She placed a spoon on the matching saucer and set the cup in front of him. Then she watched as he picked up the spoon and stirred.

"Your long fingers make my china look like something

out of a little girl's play set," Shannon blurted, immediately wishing she hadn't.

Michael quirked an eyebrow. "Oh?"

She snorted out a nervous laugh. "I mean, next to your hand it appears tiny. I wasn't implying that you play with dolls ..." *Och! What is the matter with me?*

"Well," Michael shifted awkwardly in his chair, "that's a relief."

Shannon avoided his gaze for a few moments, focusing on preparing her own cup of tea and trying to regroup. Her cellphone beeped on the counter next to her, indicating she had a text message, and she welcomed the momentary diversion.

"Excuse me for one second," she said as she reached for the phone.

She hit the "Messages" icon and a text message from Coleen popped up on the screen. Big and bold, it read: "I MEANT TO ASK YOU, IS THAT MICHAEL STONE STILL AS DEVILISHLY HANDSOME AS I REMEMBER???"

"Och!" Shannon muttered and quickly tried to delete the message. In her haste, her hand fumbled and the cellphone shot out of her fingers. She watched with horror as it sailed through the air ... and landed in Michael's hand.

Leave it to Coleen!

"Everything OK?" he asked, opening his hand to peer down at the phone.

"Fine," she said, and leaned across the counter to snatch it out of his hand before he could get a good look at the screen. Determined to deal with it later, she shoved it in her pocket.

After a few calming gulps of her tea, she peered at Michael over the rim of her cup. "I really appreciate you coming here to discuss Paul Wilson with me," she said.

"I have to warn you, I have ulterior motives." He held her gaze and she felt that little zing of attraction she tried so hard to ignore.

"What motive might that be?" she asked, not entirely sure she wanted to know the answer.

"When you told me on the phone you'd gone to Portland Aviation, I felt a need to warn you that you could be treading on dangerous ground." Michael paused. "You're in over your head with this."

"Oh." Her hope that he might be able to help her deflated like a pierced balloon.

"Hey." Michael reached out his hand as if to comfort her, and then let it fall short. "I don't mean to hurt your feelings. But I want to make sure you understand the risks you're taking."

She reached for her keys and dangled the can of pepper spray in front of him. "Don't worry about me. I'm taking precautions."

"That's good," he said patiently. "But pepper spray doesn't protect you from everything. If it did, cops wouldn't need to carry guns." He grinned that sweet little lopsided number she liked so much.

"I suppose you have a point." She fidgeted with her cup.

He sighed. "I'm not going to convince you to give up this investigation, am I?"

"No. Melanie is counting on me, and I don't want to let her down."

"There's nothing more admirable than helping a friend,"

Michael said. "I'll tell you what. I'll back off if you agree to give me a heads-up on all future plans that involve tracking down Edward's killer. At least that way, if I can't talk you out of doing whatever it is you're planning, I can advise you on how to best stay safe. Deal?"

Shannon couldn't stop the smile that spread across her face. "It's a deal."

"Good." He took another sip of his tea. She saw his mouth pucker slightly as he swallowed the amber liquid, but he quickly recovered. "Now, about Paul Wilson ..."

"You mentioned on the phone you had some ideas about what he might want to cover up."

Michael nodded. "My first thought is he's violating FAA regulations and Edward caught him in the act."

"Regulations such as?"

"Falsifying equipment maintenance records. Using substandard parts for repairs. Pilot hour violations, etc."

"Is there a way I can find out if he's on the FAA's hit list?"

"They don't keep a public database, if that's what you're asking, but I know people who could look into it for you."

The way he'd said *people* sent a bolt of uneasiness through her. "People? Like who, specifically?"

"Associates," he answered vaguely. "It's also possible that Paul is involved in transporting illegal goods, or even people who are evading the law."

"True." Shannon noted how quickly Michael had changed the subject to avoid directly answering her question. *This time, I'll let it slide.* "Could you find out if he has a record?"

"Yes, but he doesn't need to have a record to be involved in illegal activities."

"I understand, but it would make it more likely, right?"

"It could," Michael said.

"What about environmental issues?"

"Environmental?" he asked, clearly surprised. "As in related to his business?"

She nodded. "Edward was doing Internet searches for the FAA and coastal pollution on the same day. I'm wondering if there's any chance his business could be polluting."

Michael considered it for a few moments. "There are chemicals involved in operating a fleet of choppers," he said. "I suppose he could be dumping them instead of properly disposing of them."

"I thought the same thing."

"I can research the FAA violations for you, but if Paul's polluting, you'll have to catch him in the act." Michael fixed a hard stare on her. "And if I can't talk you out of doing that, then remember, you agreed to call me before acting."

Shannon bristled at his bossy tone. "I remember our deal, but it doesn't mean you get to order me around like a drill sergeant."

He met her challenging gaze. "I was merely re-stating the factual terms of our verbal agreement for clarification purposes."

The man is truly hopeless! "Thank you for that, but the clarification was unnecessary—*I'm* not that easily confused," she said, smiling sweetly. "Anyway, I do appreciate your willingness to help."

Michael nodded.

Shannon pointed at his barely touched cup. "Not crazy about it?"

"No offense, but I think I'll stick to coffee." He softened his words with a disarming smile. "I'd better get going."

"OK." Shannon slipped off her stool. "Thanks again for coming by."

"Any time." He stood and took a few steps toward the door, then turned. "Be careful, Shannon. You're dealing with a very dangerous person." Bells above the front door jingled, and Melanie walked in.

"I promise I'll be careful," Shannon replied, offering a mock salute. "*Sir.*"

He shook his head and turned away. As he passed Melanie, he nodded a greeting.

Through the window, Shannon watched him cross the street. "Do you feel like ordering a pizza and looking through more of Edward's records?" she asked absently.

"Sure."

Shannon pulled her gaze from the window. "I have a few things to do before I can leave. I'll order the pizza, and we can meet at my place in an hour."

Melanie jangled her keys. "And then you'll tell me about your trip to Portland?'

"Absolutely."

"OK, then I won't overwhelm you with questions now," Melanie said. "I'll see you at your place soon."

Melanie exited the store, and Shannon turned the deadbolt behind her friend. She switched to autopilot, quickly working through store-closing procedures and ending with a phone call to her favorite pizza place. As she walked the store aisles one last time, she mentally ticked off the closing steps to be sure she'd completed everything. Satisfied, she headed for her truck.

Once on the road, an uneasy feeling crept over her. She checked her rearview mirror to see if someone was tailing her, but all she saw were dark clouds off the coast, a sure sign of impending rain.

I'm letting the letter get to me. I have to get a grip. But the feeling wouldn't leave her. Even when she pulled into the driveway where Melanie waited, unease kept her attentive to her surroundings.

She hopped out of her truck and rushed toward her friend. "Hey, Mel, do you think I could get that pepper spray back from you?"

A look of alarm flashed over Melanie's face. "Why? Did something happen?"

"No," Shannon said, hurrying up the steps. "But Michael keeps telling me to be careful, and even though he does it in a bossy, slightly maddening sort of way, I figured I'd better heed his warning."

"Good thinking." Melanie snapped the container free.

Shannon reached for the spray just as a vehicle zoomed into view at the end of the long drive. "Hurry, we need to get inside," she said. She raced to the front door and fumbled with the keys in her haste to find the right one.

"Who is that?" Melanie asked.

"I don't know. C'mon!" Shannon finally found the right key and opened the door. She turned to find her friend still standing in the driveway. "Mel!"

"It's the pizza guy," Melanie announced, still rooted in place.

As the car drew closer, Shannon could see the large pizza decal on the hood.

"What's gotten into you?" Melanie asked.

"I thought he was tailing me."

"He probably was. There aren't too many ways to get out here from town."

Shannon hissed out a breath and waited for the driver to join them.

Once on the steps, the driver held up his free arm and nodded at the pepper spray in Shannon's hand. "No need to use that on me, I'm just the delivery guy."

Melanie mocked a serious look. "Sorry, but if there aren't any mushrooms on that pizza, *I'll* have to use it on you."

"Phew." He swiped a hand across his forehead. "Good thing it's loaded with them."

Shannon chuckled, feeling the tension drain from her shoulders. She handed him a tip, then led the way into the kitchen. "I'll get drinks."

Melanie headed straight to the refrigerator. "Oh, good. You still have cheesecake."

"I thought with everything going on right now, you might need your favorite dessert, so I didn't take it to the senior center with the rest of the goodies," Shannon said.

"You're right. I'm cutting myself a huge piece." She set a pitcher of iced tea on the island and then added the cheesecake.

Shannon put two slices of gooey pepperoni, mushroom, and cheese pizza on a plate. "Let's eat in the dining room," she suggested. "It will give us plenty of space to spread out so we can look through Ed's records at the same time."

"Really? I thought Deborah liked to keep the table set." Melanie started pouring tea into tall glasses.

"She did. But every time I went in there, I was afraid I'd knock something on the floor, so I asked her to put the formal dishes away." Shannon picked up her plate. "I'll meet you in there."

On the way, Shannon made a detour into the study and grabbed the file that contained Edward's records. Back in the dining room, she took out the records still to be reviewed and split them into two piles. She set one stack next to an empty chair for Melanie and kept the other for herself.

Melanie returned carrying two small dessert plates topped with large slices of cheesecake. "I decided you'll have to join me in having dessert," she said. "I'm not going to be the only one consuming all these calories."

Shannon feigned distress, holding the back of her hand against her forehead. "I suppose if I have to sacrifice myself for my friend, I can do so."

Melanie laughed as she took a seat. The happy sound brightened Shannon's outlook.

"Exactly what is it we're looking for here?" Melanie asked as she chomped off the tip of her pizza slice.

"I'm not sure. Anything that seems out of place." Shannon examined a credit card statement from the previous month. "A reoccurring charge, perhaps. Or any expense that seems odd for Edward."

"You mean like this one for a spa?" Melanie snorted as she slid the top page across the table. "Ed wouldn't be caught dead at a spa."

Shannon looked up in time to see Melanie's mouth form a perfect O.

"I can't believe I just said that," Melanie whispered and an awkward silence hung in the air. "I wasn't making light of his death. You know that, right?"

"Of course," Shannon said quickly. "Um ... perhaps the spa charge was for Angie."

"Or he could've been cheating on Angie," Melanie said, her voice turning bitter. "And this is for yet another girlfriend."

"If we find more of these charges, I'll make a note to ask Angie about it."

They ate and searched through records in silence, finishing off the pizza and moving on to the cheesecake.

Melanie took a large bite and groaned with delight. "This is truly the best cheesecake I've ever eaten. You should serve it in the coffee shop when it opens."

"I could, I suppose," Shannon mused. "It will depend on the equipment I decide to install."

"You could bake it here."

"Not if I want to meet health codes. Now what's this?" Shannon picked up a copied receipt and double-checked to be sure she was seeing what she thought she was seeing. Excited, she handed the paper to Melanie. "Take a look."

Melanie studied it. "Morgan Lombardi had lunch with Ed. I wonder why?"

Shannon wondered the same thing. The last person she'd expected to see turn up in her search was Morgan, the disgruntled ex-manager of the Paisley Craft Market & Artist Lofts. But Edward had scribbled her name on a restaurant receipt that had been time-stamped at 12:20 p.m. one day during the previous week. "Do you think she was involved in some kind of scheme with him?"

"Perhaps," Melanie said.

Shannon thought for a moment. "Or maybe his interest in her was purely romantic."

Melanie nodded. "Knowing Ed, it's certainly possible."

"Perhaps he was two-timing her with Angie," Shannon said. "And when Morgan found out, she killed him and set it up to look like he was murdered at my store to put me out of business."

Melanie sat back and drummed her fingers on the tabletop. "I know I said she might've done it, but the more I think about it, the more murder seems too extreme for her. Plus, if Greg *does* discover money in Ed's accounts, then our theory wouldn't explain that."

"You're right. Morgan didn't have any money, so she sure couldn't have been paying him. I think it's more likely they were involved in a blackmail scheme together. I can definitely see Morgan blackmailing someone."

Melanie beamed. "So can I."

"I think we're onto a very promising lead," Shannon said, trying not to sound too excited in case it didn't pan out. "Now all we need to do is prove it."

— 12 —

Shannon closed the cash register and stifled a yawn as she said goodbye to a delightful customer from Salem who'd wandered in from the beach earlier that morning. The woman left with several jewelry pieces as well as several craft books on beading.

With the shop empty, Shannon reached for the telephone and dialed Angie's number. After five rings, Angie's voice mail picked up.

At the beep, Shannon said, "Angie, it's Shannon McClain. We spoke the other day about Edward. I'm trying to find out why he had lunch with a Morgan Lombardi. Could you call me as soon as possible?" She left her phone number and ended the call.

Her cellphone rang before she had a chance to put it away. At the sight of her best friend's picture on the screen, she hurried to answer it. "Hi, Coleen."

"Did you get my text about Michael?" Coleen asked. "You never answered it."

"I got it," Shannon replied flatly. "And what rotten timing it was. I was with him when it came through."

Coleen chuckled. "Brilliant. It sounds like the man still has you all aflutter."

"I am *not* aflutter," Shannon insisted. "Did you talk to Alec?"

"I'm sitting in my car outside his dorm right now."

Shannon would have had to have been deaf to miss the ominous tone Coleen's voice had taken. "This doesn't sound good." She pressed the phone closer to her ear as she waited to hear the details.

"It isn't, I'm afraid. I tried to pretend I was in town for other reasons, but Alec saw right through me when I dropped in."

"And?"

"And he was upset that you sent me to check on him. He asked me to tell you that he's a grown man now and can take care of himself."

Shannon sat back and sighed. "This is where you say 'I told you so.'"

"I wouldn't dream of it," Coleen said earnestly.

"Any hint as to what was bothering him?" Shannon asked, hoping that if she'd offended her son by sending Coleen to check up on him, she might at least have learned something about his problem in the process.

"Not a word. Whatever it is, he's not ready to talk about it. But on a brighter note, I'm on my way to see Lara."

A stab of jealousy pierced Shannon's heart. She longed to see her children, but she was the one who'd decided to stay in Oregon, so she was also the one who had to buck up until they arrived. "I hope you enjoy visiting with her. I'm sure she'll be happier to see you than Alec was."

"I'll give her a big hug for you," Coleen added.

"Thanks." They ended their call, and Shannon circled her arms around her stomach to ease the physical ache of missing her children. *Children.* But they weren't children anymore; they were young adults. She had to get used to thinking like that and give them some space.

The bells above the door jangled, and Melanie slipped in. When they'd parted the previous night, Melanie had been upbeat and cheerful about the new lead. But now her expression looked drawn and worried. Even the vibrant orange shirt she wore couldn't brighten her downtrodden appearance, and Shannon's worry over Alec was replaced by concern for her friend.

"What's wrong?" Shannon asked as she walked around the counter.

"Grayson." Melanie spit out his name like a bitter pill. "He asked me to come to the station as soon as possible."

Oh, no, Shannon thought, struggling to keep her expression from displaying her fear. "Did he say why he wanted to see you?"

"No, but I'm afraid he's going to arrest me." Fear, stark and vivid, glittered in Melanie's eyes.

Shannon grasped Melanie's hand and held tight. "Don't panic. More than likely, he just has a few more questions to ask you."

Melanie's hand trembled in Shannon's grasp. "Will you come with me?" she asked.

"Of course. Let me tell Essie where I'm going, and then we'll leave." Shannon drew Melanie toward a stool and urged her to sit. "I'll be right back."

Shannon found Essie on a ladder near the rear of the stockroom. "I hate to say this, but I have to go out for a few minutes. Can you man the sales floor?"

"Is everything OK?" Essie asked.

With Melanie's impending arrest, Shannon could no longer keep the dismay from her tone. "I hope so."

Essie searched Shannon's face, but when Shannon didn't share any details, Essie finally nodded and started climbing down. "I'm right behind you."

"Thanks, Essie." Shannon grabbed her jacket and purse from the office and joined Melanie, who was chewing her lip as if her life depended on it. "We can go now."

She linked her arm with Melanie's and led her outside before Essie could ask any more questions.

On the sidewalk, a blustery wind caught Shannon off guard, and she felt Melanie shiver. Shannon pulled her friend closer, and they hurried through the heavy gusts, which bent and twisted the flowers in the hanging baskets that lined the streets. Shannon looked at the sky; it was thick with gray clouds, threatening to open up any minute. They picked up their pace, rushing down Main Street to the police station.

Shannon had never been inside the station before, and the modern foyer caught her by surprise. A tall, padded reception desk stood in the middle of the space. An older woman sat behind it.

Shannon urged Melanie toward a chair. "You sit. I'll tell them you're here." Melanie complied without arguing—and that worried Shannon more than anything.

Shannon approached the desk and smiled at the receptionist. "Melanie Burkhart to see the chief. He's expecting us."

"I'll let him know you're here." The receptionist punched a button on her phone, and after saying Melanie had arrived, she listened intently before hanging up. "The chief may be a while, so go ahead and have a seat, Melanie."

Shannon didn't bother correcting the receptionist's mistake about her identity, but joined Melanie in the waiting area.

Melanie shifted to face her. "Promise me something," she said solemnly, as the howling wind thrust stinging sand at the window behind them.

"Anything."

"If Grayson *does* arrest me, don't tell Greg. It'd be too much for him to deal with right now."

Shannon blinked. "But he has to know."

"No he doesn't."

"What if he tries to call you?"

"I can phone him and tell him I won't be in cell range and to leave me a message."

Shannon shook her head. "He'll hear about your arrest on the news. Is that how you want him to find out?"

"Just promise me!" Melanie exclaimed, drawing a wary look from the receptionist.

Shannon saw the wild look in Melanie's eyes and knew her friend was not thinking clearly. "Let's not talk about this unless we have to, OK?"

Melanie didn't respond. She studied Shannon closely, a strange expression on her face. "Sometimes I marvel at how you can be so sure of my innocence. What would you think of me if it turned out that I did kill Ed?"

Shannon blinked. "Why would you say something like that?"

"The way the evidence keeps stacking up against me, *I'm* starting to think I may have done it. I have been known to sleepwalk."

Shannon saw the receptionist lean in their direction, blatantly eavesdropping. "Do *not* say another word out here, Mel. The stress of this is getting to you and you're talking nonsense."

"Melanie. Shannon." Grayson's voice boomed from across the room. They snapped their heads in his direction. "Come on back to the conference room, Melanie."

Shannon jumped up. "I'm coming with her, and before you say no, it's not negotiable."

He gave her an irritated look. She squared her shoulders and waited for him to argue, but he simply gestured for them to follow him. He led the way into a windowless room. The dim space added to Shannon's already dark mood, and she could only imagine what the gloomy room was doing to Melanie— the woman was clearly hanging on by a thread as it was.

Grayson pointed to a table with thickly padded chairs. "Please have a seat."

Shannon and Melanie sat next to each other, sinking into cushions that let out a wheeze under their weight. Shannon shrugged off her coat and helped Melanie out of hers.

The chief took a seat facing them. "What can you tell me about the oleander plant, Melanie?"

"Oleander?" She blinked. "You called me here to talk about plants?"

He nodded. "I figure since you work at The Flower Pot, you might know something about oleander."

"I'm no expert," Melanie said cautiously, "but I do know the plant likes to grow in sandy soils. And I guess the biggest thing is that it's extremely poisonous. Ingestion of a single leaf can kill a child. I—"

Poison? Shannon squeezed Melanie's arm to stop her from talking.

"Ouch." Melanie rubbed her arm and looked at Shannon.

"Was that what killed Edward?" Shannon asked.

He gave a single nod, eyes still fixed on Melanie.

"You think because I know it's poisonous, that proves I should be your top suspect?" Melanie asked incredulously.

"I'm afraid so. I've also learned that the yarn we found binding Ed's wrists is the same yarn you're using to make a sweater for your son, Greg." The chief glanced briefly at Shannon. "A fact I suspect *you* knew but failed to tell me."

Shannon was careful to keep her expression blank. *Who would have told him about the yarn?*

Melanie shifted in her chair but didn't speak.

Grayson continued, "The fact is, this is sufficient information to get a warrant to search your home and car."

Melanie looked like an animal trapped in headlights. She drew in a deep breath and let it out. "Fine. Go ahead and search it."

"That's not a good idea, Melanie," Shannon said, laying her hand over Melanie's. "Not without a warrant anyway."

Grayson gave Shannon a sour look. "If you don't have anything to hide, Melanie, then it should be no problem."

"I *don't* have anything to hide. We can go right now if you want to."

"Melanie, stop," Shannon warned.

"Why?" Melanie asked. "I'm innocent, and they won't find anything that says otherwise."

"I need to talk to you in private," Shannon insisted. Then turning to Grayson she said, "Please excuse us for a minute." She pulled Melanie to her feet and dragged her out of the room, into the narrow hallway.

"Don't willingly give Grayson access to your home or your car," Shannon whispered. "You never know what he'll find that he can use against you."

Melanie crossed her arms. "Since I didn't kill Ed, Grayson won't find anything to prove that I did."

Shannon eased closer. "Edward has ridden in your car. He's lived in your house. They could find something he left behind and use it to say he was with you that night."

Melanie perched a hand on her hip. "You know I threw out everything Ed left behind. And I may not keep my car as spotless as you do, but I *have* cleaned it since we split up."

"All it takes is a single strand of hair to get DNA that they could use as evidence," Shannon pleaded.

Melanie rolled her eyes. "You watch too much television."

"You asked for my help. Please take my advice on this, and don't let Grayson search your car or house without a warrant. Buy yourself more time!"

Melanie opened her mouth to argue but then snapped it closed. She slowly nodded. "Fine."

They returned to the interrogation room and found Grayson sitting with his elbows resting on the table, his fingers holding his chin as if he were too weary to hold up his head. "Are you finished filling her head with nonsense, Shannon?"

"You'll have to get that warrant," Melanie said. She sounded tough and resolved, but she still looked as if a strong wind could blow her over.

"Have it your way." The chief stood, his chair scraping against the tile floor. "I'll see you both out."

"You know, Grayson," Shannon said as she handed Melanie her coat, "there are plenty of other people in town who might be familiar with oleander."

"Like who?"

As they walked down the hallway, Shannon thought about the residents she'd met in her short time in Apple Grove. "What about Elaina at The Flower Pot?"

He raised a brow. "What motive might she have to kill Ed?"

Shannon opened her mouth to say something, but nothing came to mind. For all she knew, Elaina didn't even know Edward, much less have a reason to kill him.

"It's not as easy to solve a murder as you thought, huh?" Grayson's lips curled in a smirk.

"Actually, I'm not at all surprised you're having trouble with this case," Shannon snapped. "You're focused on the wrong suspect."

She caught up to Melanie on the sidewalk. Ominous clouds still hung in the sky, typical for the season. They were a perfect reflection of Shannon's mood. Fortunately, the black clouds hadn't erupted—at least not yet.

They needed to take cover before the storm broke. Shannon grabbed Melanie's arm and urged her toward her car. Her friend dawdled so Shannon pulled harder.

"Wait, slow down. I can't keep up." Melanie jerked free of Shannon's grasp.

Shannon stopped and faced her friend, who appeared lost and confused. Shannon figured she'd feel the same way if she'd just been told the police wanted to search her home. "Sorry, Mel, but we don't have a second to waste."

"A second of what? My freedom?" Melanie clutched her chest as if Shannon had stabbed her with a knife.

"No, of course not." Shannon softened her tone. "A second of time before heading to your house to do our own search and make sure Grayson won't find anything."

"I *told* you, I got rid of all of Ed's things."

Shannon struggled to remain patient. "Right, but if someone is truly framing you for his murder, then they may have planted something at the same time they took your knitting needle."

A sharp gust of wind seemed to knock Melanie off balance. "Oh, this wind is terrible!" She quickly grabbed onto a lamppost. "Don't you think I would've noticed something out of place?" she insisted.

Shannon planted her feet a few feet apart to withstand the forces beating against her back. "Did you notice the needle was missing?"

"No, but—" Melanie's voice drifted away on a current of air, and she chewed her lip again. "You're right. We'd better check."

"You drive, and I'll call Michael on the way. He should be able to tell us what Grayson might be looking for."

Shannon pulled Melanie close, and with their heads down, they battled the wind all the way to Melanie's SUV. Once inside, Shannon combed her fingers through her knotted hair, dug out her cellphone, and dialed Michael. *The way things are going with this investigation, I should probably put him on speed dial.*

Michael answered on the second ring. "Shannon, is everything OK?"

As Melanie navigated the streets of Apple Grove, gripping the wheel tightly, Shannon told him about their meeting at the police station. The words flew from her mouth in a long, nervous ramble.

"So I need to know, what do you think he's looking for?" Shannon finished.

"First of all, take a deep breath," Michael said. "And second, it will be simpler if I meet you at Melanie's house to do the search myself."

Her heart warmed at his willingness to help again. "You're sure?"

"I'm sure."

"Thank you." Shannon disconnected and turned to Melanie. "He's coming over to do a search himself."

"I guessed as much from the flush on your cheeks."

"What?" Shannon pulled down the visor mirror and saw the bright red splotches coloring her pale complexion. "That's from arguing with Grayson."

Melanie said nothing, but concentrated on her driving.

As Melanie turned onto her street, which was lined with small cottages overlooking the beach, Shannon pondered what Grayson might find at the house. He knew about the yarn, so other than taking a sample to match it, that was a nonissue. Likely, he would focus on the oleander.

Shannon remembered a show she'd recently seen where a woman was poisoned by her husband, and how the police had found searches on his computer for the poison. *Could the killer have used Melanie's computer to perform such a search and make it look like Melanie had researched poisonous plants?*

As she turned to Melanie, she caught sight of the ocean swells breaking harshly on the beach. "We'll need to check your computer to make sure there're no searches related to oleander."

"No need," Melanie said. "I never searched for poisons."

"Remember, we're dealing with a criminal who's trying to frame you. That person could've used your computer to make it *look* like you searched for it."

Melanie shivered. "It's so creepy to think someone was in my house. After all of this, I don't know if I can stay there alone."

"Maybe you should stay with me until this is resolved," Shannon suggested.

Melanie shook her head. "I don't want to put you out any more than I already have."

"Put me out? I have six empty bedrooms! It's about time at least one of them is put to good use."

The hint of a smile played on Melanie's lips. "OK, fine. Thank you."

"You can pack a bag while I search your computer."

Fat drops of rain plopped onto the windshield as they pulled into the driveway. They jumped out of the SUV and ran to the porch. Once inside, they took off their jackets and shook them over the rug.

"Where is your computer?" Shannon asked.

"In my craft room." Melanie flipped on a light. It did little to battle the gloom. She led the way to the back of the house and into the craft room. The room had a cheerful decor, with creamy taupe walls and flowery curtains on windows, and it overlooked a tidy backyard. Shannon saw Melanie's perennials bending to the ground in the fierce wind. She wondered if they'd ever stand up again. *Is this a sign of what's to come for Melanie?*

Melanie pressed a button on the computer, and the machine whirred in response.

Shannon sat down in an oak chair boasting a flowery needlepoint cushion. "Do you have a password?"

Melanie shook her head. "I never thought I'd need one, but now I'm wishing I'd used one."

Dread filled Shannon. "You go pack that bag. I'll handle this and let Michael in when he arrives."

Melanie left the room without comment.

When the computer dinged in readiness, Shannon clicked on the browser's history tab. She scrolled back a few weeks and scanned the links visited. Most of the links favored crafting sites. As she neared the bottom, she spotted a search for poisonous plants, and her hand fell away from the mouse.

Right below the search was a link with "oleander" in the title. There it was. The poison that had killed Edward, big and bold for the police to see when they arrived.

13

"You can't delete the searches, Melanie," Michael said from his seat at the table in her cramped dining room. "Deleting them would be considered obstructing justice. Besides, clearing your history doesn't make it go away. A computer forensic expert could restore the file, and that would make you look even guiltier."

Melanie sighed and slumped back in her chair. "Then what can I do?"

Michael seemed reluctant to answer Melanie's question.

"Tell me," she pressed. "I need to know what you honestly think."

"I think you need to hire a good criminal defense attorney," he said.

"Oh, this can't be happening." Melanie shot to her feet and began to pace in front of the window. "I'm going to jail. This is unbelievable. I'm going to jail!"

"I didn't say that," Michael said. "But I want to make sure if something does happen, you'll have a representative on call."

Shannon joined her friend, pacing alongside her. "Keep in mind that Grayson doesn't know about the computer search, and that gives us more time to find the real killer."

"But we don't have anything solid to go on," Melanie said. "All we have are theories."

"Tell me what you've discovered so far. Perhaps I can suggest a strategy," Michael offered.

"Good idea. Let's do that," Shannon agreed, guiding Melanie back to the table. Once she sat down, Shannon dug out a pad of paper and pen from her purse. "Give me a minute to jot everything down so I don't forget anything. Then we can discuss it." She wrote "Clues and Suspects" at the top of a page and remembered Michael's means, motives and opportunities advice. "Let's start with motive."

Melanie's phone rang from where it sat on the table, and she glanced at the screen. "It's Greg. Excuse me."

Shannon waited for Melanie to leave the room, then peered at Michael. "It doesn't look good for her, does it?" she whispered.

He shook his head. "I didn't want to mention this in front of Melanie, but as I was looking at the history on her computer, I noted the searches were made shortly before Edward was killed."

"So it's likely that at the same time the killer broke in to get the knitting needle, he also searched her computer."

"Yes, but that's not the worst bit of news. Grayson can also use this to call into question Melanie's whereabouts at the time Edward was murdered. She couldn't be on her nightly walk at the same time as she was searching her computer." He met Shannon's worried gaze. "We both know Melanie didn't do this, but Grayson will think she lied about her alibi, and he's bound to wonder what else she's lied about."

"All the more reason to get to the bottom of this quickly," Shannon said as she resumed jotting down items on her suspect list. Michael moved in closer to read over her shoulder.

Paul Wilson: Motive—Hide wrongdoing for which Edward was blackmailing him.

Morgan: Motive—Get back at Shannon for ruining her job and/or participating in blackmailing Edward's boss.

Angie's ex-boyfriend Buddy: Motive—Upset over their breakup.

Once finished, she looked up to find Michael watching her.

"About number one," he said. "Do you have any solid proof Edward was blackmailing someone?"

She shook her head. "Greg is trying to get Edward's financial records to see if he came into any money. Maybe that's why he's calling Melanie."

"Let's hope so." Michael tapped his index finger on the second item on the list. "I can help with this one. When we finish here, I'll put pressure on my contact at the FAA. We need to know if Edward reported Portland Aviation. I've already asked him to look into Ocean Tours. Edward may not be working for them anymore, but if he was blackmailing someone, it could go back to his time there."

Shannon nodded, thankful to have Michael on their side. "Good thinking," she said.

Melanie returned and slipped into her chair. "Greg finally got copies of Ed's bank statements. He's been depositing $5,000 in cash every month for the last seven months." A broad smile crept across her face.

Shannon matched her grin. "Blackmail money."

"Possibly," Michael said. "My gut says you're on to something. But it could simply be that he was working as a pilot on the side and they paid him in cash."

"But his girlfriend said he didn't work long hours," Shannon said. "And besides, what legal activity could he be doing that would make that much money each month?"

"Plus," Melanie jumped in, "he doesn't own a helicopter or a plane."

Michael shrugged. "Maybe he was using company equipment after hours, and *he* was the one violating FAA standards. Then he looked up the rules to see what he needed to do to cover his tracks."

"Sounds like a theory we need to add to our list," Shannon said, jotting the information onto her notepad. She tapped her pen on Buddy's name next to motive theory number three. "After learning about the cash deposits in Edward's account, this one seems less likely."

"Don't be so quick to dismiss it," Michael warned. "Edward's death and the fact that he might've been blackmailing someone or working for cash don't have to be related."

Shannon thought about Michael's comment. He was right. They couldn't rule out anything yet. They had to follow up on all leads. "I'll start with Buddy tomorrow," she said. "If he has an alibi for the night Edward was killed, then we can rule him out, and I'll go see Paul Wilson again."

"I'm going with you to talk to Buddy." Michael's blue eyes met Shannon's, and she could tell by his expression that he wouldn't back down until she agreed to let him accompany her.

"Fine," she said. Truth be told, she was grateful to have someone by her side that possessed the skills needed to subdue a killer.

*   *   *

The next morning broke clear and sunny. Shannon sat in the passenger seat of Michael's sleek Lexus and tried to hide her frustration. She'd asked him a few more personal questions, attempting to get to know him on a deeper level as they made the drive to Portland, but he'd managed to sidestep every one of them with vague answers—even though he'd told her less than a week before that if she wanted to know *anything* about him, all she had to do was ask.

By the time he made the turn onto Buddy's tree-lined street, Shannon knew little more about him than when she'd settled into his car an hour earlier.

Although Buddy's neighborhood wasn't completely run-down, it wasn't up to the standards of most Portland neighborhoods. When they pulled up behind a broken-down car, Shannon was thankful to have Michael sitting next to her.

He turned off the engine and faced her. "I'll go up the walk first," he said. "You stay behind me. Follow my lead, and if I tell you to return to the car, do it immediately. No questions asked. Got it?"

Though she didn't appreciate being ordered about, she gave in to the wave of unease that tumbled through her. "OK. And for the record, you're scaring me a little," she said.

"Sorry. I don't anticipate any trouble, but it's better to be prepared." He smiled, a dimple peeking from his cheek. "All set?"

"Let's go," she said and slipped out of his car.

She followed him up a crumbling sidewalk lined with dried brown weeds curling down to meet the wet soil. The sun heated her back, but she still felt chilled inside from

Michael's warning. He stepped onto the dilapidated porch with a sagging wooden floor and pounded on the door.

He opened his mouth as if to speak, then snapped it closed.

"What?" she whispered.

"Nothing." He gave a quick shake of his head. "Old habits die hard. I almost yelled 'Police!'"

As they stood waiting for someone to answer, she seized the chance to find out more about him. "Do you miss being an officer?"

"Miss it?" He seemed truly surprised by her question. "Not most of it, but I did like the satisfaction of solving a crime."

Shannon smiled. "Then you must be really happy to be with me this morning—I mean happy that I asked you to help me solve this case so you could come with me, here. Well, technically I came with you in your car ..." *I'm rambling like an idiot on the front porch of a suspected psychopath! What is wrong with me?*

Michael's confused expression mirrored her thoughts. Fortunately, the door swung open and jerked his attention away from her. A thin man with long hair and a beard stood in the doorway. His eyes darted back and forth between them, appearing as though he might flee at any moment.

"Are you Buddy?" Shannon asked.

The man eyed her suspiciously. "Who wants to know?"

"I'm a friend of Angie's."

He switched his focus to Michael. "Who are you?"

"Another friend."

The man scoffed. "If she's filing a harassment complaint against Buddy, tell her there's no point. He won't be bothering her again for a few years."

"I don't follow," Shannon said, drawing the guy's attention back to her.

"He was busted for possession with intent a week or so ago. Been in lockup ever since."

"Really," she said, quickly processing the fact that if Buddy was incarcerated, he couldn't have killed Edward. She'd finally made an inch of progress in her case. It wasn't a good development, but she'd moved forward nonetheless. "I'm sure Angie will be relieved to hear that."

"Good for Angie. I need to find another roommate to make the rent payment." The man looked at Michael, then back at Shannon. "You need anything else, or can I get back to my video game?"

"We're done here," Michael said, gesturing for Shannon to precede him down the stairs. But he didn't take his eyes off the guy.

The door slammed shut, sending a puff of paint chips into the air, and Shannon hurried back to the car. With Buddy officially off the suspect list, she planned to switch her focus to Portland Aviation.

Michael held the car door open for her. "Do you want to stop by Portland Aviation before heading out of the city?"

"You read my mind. But I hate to impose on you," she said.

"I'm happy to help you."

She suppressed a smile, touched that he would give up his entire day for her. "If you're sure it's no trouble."

Michael flashed his lopsided grin. "To tell you the truth, it feels really good working a crime again."

Feeling a sting of disappointment, she slid into the car. *Mental note—stop acting like a giddy schoolgirl. He misses the thrill of his old job. That's the only reason he's being so helpful.*

Michael's cellphone rang and she watched him answer it as he ran around the front of the car. Once behind the wheel, he listened, drumming his fingers on his knee.

"What about Ocean Tours in Apple Grove?" he asked. "OK, thanks for the update, Dave." He ended the call and settled his phone in a dashboard holder. "That was my contact at the FAA. There are no violations on Portland Aviation's record, but Ocean Tours is another matter. They have a long history of maintenance violations and are on probationary status. One more problem and the FAA will shut them down."

The spark of excitement that lit in Shannon's stomach every time she found a clue took flame. "If Edward caught them in a violation, he may have demanded money in lieu of reporting them to the FAA," she said.

"Sounds likely."

"Then maybe we should head back to Apple Grove instead of going to Portland Aviation."

"We're already here. It wouldn't hurt to see if Paul Wilson knows anything about Morgan and Edward," he suggested.

Shannon couldn't wait to get going. "We can start by questioning the receptionist. She's very talkative."

"Let's do it." Michael cranked the engine, and after checking his mirrors, he eased onto the road behind a small electric car. "You don't happen to have a picture of Morgan do you?"

"No, why?"

"This receptionist may not know Morgan by name, but she might recognize a photo of her."

Shannon pulled out her phone. "After Morgan quit, I shoved a photo of her and my grandmother into the credenza. I could get Essie to snap a picture of it on her cellphone and send it to me."

He glanced at her. "I'm surprised that after learning what Morgan did, you didn't trash it."

"I'm having a hard time getting rid of anything that belonged to my grandmother," Shannon replied. Not wanting to talk about it any farther, she dialed Essie.

"Paisley Craft Market, Essie speaking," she answered joyfully, once again reinforcing to Shannon that Essie was a gem of an employee.

"Hey, Essie, it's Shannon. There's a photo in the office credenza of Morgan and my grandmother. Can you take a picture of it with your phone and text it to me ASAP?"

"Morgan? Oh my gosh, do you think she's involved in Edward's death somehow?"

"I don't have time to go into it now," Shannon said. "Could you please send the picture? I'll fill you in when I get back to town."

"Sure."

After hanging up, Shannon watched out the window as Michael navigated the Portland roads. She admired the flowering perennials starting to unfurl next to rhododendrons and azaleas that had already lost their intensity.

When they stopped at a light, she spotted a food cart labeled "Gourmet on the Go." As recognition dawned, Shannon sucked in a sharp breath, but she kept her eyes on the cart in case her mother made an appearance. She owned several food carts, and Shannon hadn't even considered the possibility of randomly catching sight of her mother while in town.

"Everything OK?" Michael asked.

"Fine." Shannon's fingers twisted the fine chain of her locket. She didn't want to discuss her turmoil over coming to grips with a mother who'd missed most of her life—and not only her life, but her children's as well. They hadn't known their grandmother, just as Shannon hadn't known hers.

As Michael pulled away from the light, she felt like a lightning bolt had hit her. With the twins still in Scotland, she hadn't really considered what would happen when they arrived in Oregon. She should make more of an effort to build a relationship with her mother so they could have the extended family she never had.

Her phone chimed, and she was thankful for the interruption to her thoughts. She opened the multimedia message from Essie and looked at the picture.

"A little editing, and this will be perfect," she said as she navigated to the picture-editing feature to enlarge and crop Morgan's face. When she was satisfied with her work, she saved it.

A few minutes later, Michael pulled into the Portland Aviation parking lot, and they entered the reception area together. Shannon headed straight for Bethany and greeted her with a warm smile.

"Hey, I remember you from the other day." Bethany gave Shannon a conspiratorial wink. Shannon was starting to believe Bethany liked keeping secrets from her boss.

"Is Paul in?" Shannon asked, leaning casually on the ledge.

"Nah. He's out somewhere, as usual." Bethany's gaze

strayed to Michael, and she gave him an appreciative look.

Shannon stepped in front of him to regain Bethany's attention. "Would you mind taking a quick peek at a picture and telling me if you recognize someone?"

"Um ... I guess not."

Shannon held out her phone, and Bethany studied the picture of Morgan, her eyes narrowing for a moment before recognition dawned. "That's Morgan. She started working in the office a few days ago. Ed got her the job."

What? Shannon never expected the connection to be as simple as Edward helping Morgan find employment. *The lunch receipt could have been for an interview where Edward introduced her to Paul.*

Shannon's cellphone rang. She nearly dropped it before recovering and spotting Melanie's name on caller ID.

"Excuse me," she said, glancing at Michael. He stepped forward to continue the conversation with Bethany, and Shannon quickly moved to the other side of the lobby. "Hi, Melanie."

"Shannon, please, you have to get back here!" Melanie's words tumbled out in a panic. "He's in my house! What should I do?"

Shannon's stomach clutched at her friend's terrified tone. "Calm down, Mel. Who's in your house?"

"Grayson and the forensics team. They're going through everything, and he keeps talking about arresting me."

Shannon made eye contact with Michael and jerked her head toward the door. "Hold on. We'll be there as soon as we can."

14

Shannon climbed from Michael's car and cast a worried look at the vehicles surrounding Melanie's home. A tall black truck with "Oregon State Police Forensics" painted on the side took up most of the driveway, and two local police cars sat at the curb. She could only imagine how shocked Melanie must have been at their arrival. Shannon needed to get to her friend—*now*.

She ran up the walk and Michael followed close behind. At the open door, she stopped and stared inside at the chaos unfolding before her. Grayson stood like a sentry in the front room, watching his minions methodically search the space. Shannon counted four people in the room, including Grayson. One man was a local police officer dressed in uniform, and two women wore white hazmat suits.

Melanie sat in a plush chair in the corner, watching every move, pale as a ghost. She took off her glasses and rubbed her eyes. Shannon stepped forward to join her.

"Stop right there." Grayson hurried toward her. "I need you to stay outside until we've finished our search."

"I'm here to support Melanie, not destroy evidence." Shannon planted her hands on her hips and widened her stance, making it clear she wasn't going anywhere.

Michael moved closer and leaned on the doorjamb. "Grayson," he said in greeting. On the surface, Michael sounded pleasant enough, but Shannon hoped the way he stood next to her meant he had her back.

The chief nodded at Michael then turned back to Shannon. "If you insist on being here, then Melanie can join *you* on the porch."

Melanie jumped up. "Oh no. I'm not leaving you alone in my home so you can plant more evidence against me."

Grayson rolled his eyes.

"Chief!" One of the women in the white suits hurried down the hall. "You're going to want to take a look at the computer."

Shannon shared a knowing look with Melanie. Grayson noticed and raised a brow. "I need to take care of this." He trained the fierce look on Shannon that she'd come to expect from him. "Can I count on you to stay on the porch?"

"Fine."

"I'm coming with you," Melanie said.

Michael put up his hand. "Why don't you let me accompany him, Melanie?"

Shannon turned to Michael. She'd trusted him to help her; had it been the right thing to do? Or was he forever in the "brotherhood" of police officers, his loyalties ultimately with the chief?

No. If that were the case, he would have already told Grayson about the computer search, and Grayson clearly didn't know what he was about to find.

"Michael will do a good job representing you, Mel." Shannon slid her arm around Melanie's shoulder. "You can stay with me."

"OK, but I'm not going outside to the porch. I'm staying inside, where I can keep an eye on these people."

"We'll both wait here." Shannon silently pleaded with Grayson not to argue. He ignored her and marched down the hall.

Michael rested a hand on Shannon's shoulder for the briefest of moments before following Grayson. The contact may have been short, but it was long enough to confirm that he really would stand up for Melanie.

"They must've found the searches," Melanie whispered, her body trembling. "Do you think it's enough to arrest me?"

"I don't know, sweetie." Shannon hugged her closer.

Melanie shook her head as if clearing it and then stepped out from under Shannon's arm. "Please tell me you found some good news on your trip to Portland."

"Some good and some bad."

Melanie's shoulders sagged. "Give me the bad first."

"We talked to Buddy's roommate. Buddy's been in jail for a week, so he couldn't have killed Edward. And it looks like Morgan's connection to Edward is a dead end. He used his influence to get her a job at Portland Aviation."

"And the good?" Melanie asked.

"Portland Aviation had no FAA violations, but Ocean Tours has had a large number of them. So many, that if they're found in violation again, they'll lose their license."

"And you think Ed caught them doing something wrong and he blackmailed them?"

"Yes. We were on our way to talk to them when you called," Shannon said.

Melanie appeared to be somewhat encouraged. "Michael thinks this is a good lead too?" she asked.

"He does."

"That's good then, isn't it? I mean, with his law enforcement background, if he thinks it's a lead worth following, then it has to be, right?"

Shannon knew cops often thought they had strong leads, which, after further investigation, proved to be worthless. But she didn't want to add to Melanie's stress, so she held her tongue about it. "It looks promising," she said, trying to sound encouraging. "I'll head to Ocean Tours as soon as the police are done here and see what I can find out."

"Hey, Rachel," one the women investigators called out from the dining area where she knelt on the floor by her tool kit. "Check this out."

The other woman crossed the room and squatted next to her co-worker. She ran a gloved finger along a joint in the hardwood floor and flicked a glance at Melanie. Then she turned to her co-worker, and they talked in an excited whisper.

"You go, Gretchen." Rachel gave her co-worker a high-five slap. It sounded strangely hollow due to the latex gloves they both wore.

"What do you think they're doing?" Melanie shifted to get a better view.

Shannon braced herself for what she could only assume wouldn't be good news. "I don't know."

"I'll get the chief," Rachel said as she hopped up and charged down the hall.

Shannon and Melanie watched Gretchen continue to crawl around on the floor, her face inches from the wood.

Rachel soon returned, looking straight ahead. Shannon was sure they'd learned something she and Melanie wouldn't like. "The chief said to go ahead with the luminol."

Luminol? Shannon's stomach dropped

"What is it?" Melanie asked.

She didn't want to be the one to tell Melanie what it might mean. "There's no point in speculating. Let's wait to see what happens."

"You know something. Tell me." Melanie grabbed Shannon's arm. "*Please.*"

"I don't want to worry you needlessly. You have enough to think about."

"Tell me.

"Fine, I'll tell you. But don't read too much into it at this point." Shannon paused. "Luminol is used to test for blood."

"Blood!" Melanie's shout made both of the female investigators snap their heads up to stare at them.

"Shh." Shannon turned Melanie away to face the other direction.

"Oh my gosh! They think Ed was killed *here?*" Panic had taken control of Melanie's voice. "In my house? Oh, I just want out of this nightmare!"

Shannon longed to comfort her friend by denying it, but she couldn't when she was starting to think Edward had indeed lost his life under Melanie's dining table.

She tried to keep her friend calm by softly stroking her back. But when Grayson and Michael reappeared, Melanie started trembling again, and there wasn't a thing Shannon could do for her.

Michael joined Shannon and Melanie at the door, his expression grim. Grayson waited stoically by the arched entrance to the dining room.

Gretchen jerked the heavy dining room drapes closed

and retrieved a special light from a padded case that held several different battery-operated lights. Rachel turned off the overhead lights in both the dining room and the hallway. A dark pall enveloped the dining room, and Shannon's hopes faded with the light.

Both forensics investigators knelt down on the floor. Gretchen sprayed the luminol over a large area, and Rachel shone the blue light on it. Shannon couldn't see what—if anything—the light revealed.

"Well?" Grayson demanded.

Gretchen suddenly sat back. "It's blood," she announced.

Grayson's lips curled upward. He might as well have been salivating, he seemed so happy. "How did you find it?"

"I spotted a small stain when I squatted down to look for a swab in my case," Gretchen said, puffing out her chest with pride.

Grayson nodded. "Good work. Take a sample, and rush it to the lab."

"You got it." She smiled up at the chief as if he'd just awarded her the Nobel Prize.

Shannon understood the woman felt pleased that she'd done a good job, but seeing her joy infuriated her.

Grayson didn't say another word as he turned away and strutted back down the hallway. His booted feet reverberated through the tense silence until he'd disappeared from sight.

"What happens now?" Melanie whispered to Michael.

"They'll process the blood and compare it with Edward's."

"And if it matches, they'll arrest me." Melanie's voice was devoid of any hope.

"Likely." Michael stepped closer. "Have you contacted a lawyer yet?"

"No. Not that one would do me much good now."

"Hey, this isn't over by a long shot," Michael said in a gentler voice than Shannon had ever heard him use. His eyes were filled with the same warmth and compassion she'd seen the day they discovered Edward's body.

So he's not always a tough guy.

"Even if this *is* Edward's blood," he continued, "he used to live here, and it stands to reason that he might have injured himself at some point. A good lawyer will make sure a jury knows that."

"A jury?" Shannon's eyes widened. "Then you think this is headed for a trial?"

Michael nodded slowly, appearing reluctant to admit it. "First the district attorney will have to decide if the case is strong enough to prosecute, and if he does, he'll issue an arrest warrant."

"So Grayson still has to talk to the district attorney before he can arrest Melanie?" Shannon asked.

"That's right."

"How long will that take?" Shannon held her breath, fearful of the answer.

"If I were investigating this case," Michael replied, "I'd be on the phone arranging for the arrest warrant right now."

15

Melanie wobbled. Shannon feared her friend might pass out, so she sent Melanie into the family room to sit down. Due to Grayson's restrictions, Shannon couldn't even accompany her to the sofa, and she felt like she was failing her friend. *I should have worked harder to find the killer before it came to this.*

"If Grayson wasn't being so difficult, I could be with Melanie," Shannon mumbled.

"He's just doing his job," Michael said. "Let's talk on the porch for a minute." He nodded his head toward the door and stepped outside.

Michael sat on the wrought iron bench near the door, shielded from the raindrops that had started to fall. "Do you want me to call an attorney I know?" he asked.

"Would you? Melanie desperately needs an attorney and she's not making any move to find one." Shannon sat next to him, her knee bouncing nervously. "I really appreciate everything you've done to help her. I know she appreciates it too."

"I haven't done much," Michael protested quietly. "You're the one who's stood by her through all of this. I'd say you're a good friend to have."

Despite Melanie's dire circumstances, Shannon enjoyed the warm feeling his kind words gave her. "I wish I could say I've done enough, but I haven't," she said. "I should've found Ed's killer by now."

"Don't be so hard on yourself." He met her gaze and held it. "If Grayson hasn't been able to find the killer yet, how can you possibly think you should have?"

"Because Grayson is focused on Melanie, and he's not putting much effort into identifying other suspects. He's got blinders on. But I *know* she didn't kill Edward, and I *have* been looking for other leads."

"You're wrong. Grayson's following other leads too."

Shannon scoffed. "Really? Like what?"

Michael shook his head and broke their connection. "I can't share what Grayson and I talk about."

"Can you at least tell me why he's railroading Melanie like this?" Shannon challenged, her temper rising.

"Grayson is a sworn officer of the law. He can't ignore the forensic evidence in front of him." Michael paused and watched her closely. "Even if it means Melanie is arrested, I would want Grayson to follow the facts and uphold the law."

Shannon opened her mouth to argue, but just then, an SUV with a blue light bar on top pulled up and joined the other police vehicles at the street. Officer Brownley climbed out, carrying a folded piece of paper.

"Looks like you'll soon get your wish," Shannon said, her voice flat. "I assume this is the warrant?"

"Yes," Michael confirmed. "And just so we're clear, it is *not* my wish to see Melanie arrested."

"So what happens now?"

"They'll arrest Melanie and take her down to the station for booking. Then she'll go before a judge in an arraignment where bail will be set or denied."

Acid churned in Shannon's stomach. "They wouldn't deny her bail, would they?"

"This is a murder case, so yes, it's possible."

"This can't be happening—not to Melanie." Shannon tried not to panic. "Please do something, Michael. You have to stop this."

"The best thing I can do to help Melanie is call an attorney for her," Michael said, nodding at Officer Brownley as he came up the walk.

"Then do it. And hurry, please!" Shannon didn't care if she was allowed in the house or not. She jumped up and ran straight to Melanie. "Michael's calling an attorney," she announced.

Brownley stepped through the doorway. "Chief?" he called out.

"He's in the back," Gretchen offered, still seated on the dining room floor.

"Thanks." Brownley tipped his cap in greeting and headed down the hallway.

"He has the warrant, doesn't he?" Melanie asked Shannon. "I think so."

"I'm going to jail." Melanie's voice was tight. Suddenly she let out a hysterical laugh. "You can put those words on the list of things I never thought I'd say."

"I'm sure the lawyer will get you out as soon as possible," Shannon said, choosing to ignore what Michael had told her about the possibility of bail being denied. "I'm going to head over to Ocean Tours to see what I can find out." Shannon glanced at the clock. "Do you think someone will still be there?"

"Maybe," Melanie said. "The owner, Hank Gilliam, often stayed late when Ed worked there."

Officer Brownley and Grayson entered the room. The chief's focus locked on Melanie. Shannon's stomach twisted in a tight knot, and she felt like she might throw up. *How must Melanie be feeling?*

"Go ahead, Brownley," Grayson said.

Brownley pulled handcuffs from his belt and crossed the room. "Melanie Burkhart, you're under arrest for the murder of Edward Burkhart. Please stand and put your hands behind your back. You have the right to remain silent ..."

"Oh my gosh—Shannon!" Melanie grabbed Shannon's hand. "They're doing it. They're really doing it!"

"Come on, Grayson," Shannon said, her voice trembling. "It's not necessary to cuff her, is it?"

"It's procedure," Grayson replied.

Officer Brownley grabbed Melanie's arms, and snapped the cuffs around her wrists with a decisive click.

The chief approached Melanie, a surprising hint of kindness in his eye. "We're not quite finished with our search. Is there someone you want to ask to lock up after us?"

Melanie's eyes flew to Shannon's. "Will you do it?"

Shannon would do anything Melanie asked, but going to see Hank Gilliam seemed like a better use of her time. "I really need to go talk to that person we discussed earlier."

"This first, please," Melanie pleaded. "You're the only one I trust to make sure they don't set me up somehow."

Grayson let out an exasperated sigh, and Shannon had to agree with his assessment. She doubted he or his men would plant evidence. But it was important to Melanie, so she'd do as her friend wished.

"Of course I'll stay."

Grayson glared at her. "You're confined to this room, Shannon. No wandering around the house. Got it?"

"Yes."

"My house keys are in my purse," Melanie called out as Officer Brownley urged her forward with a hold on her cuffed hands.

Feeling lost, Shannon trailed them to the door like a puppy.

On the porch, Michael stepped in front of Melanie, stopping the procession. "I've arranged for an attorney to meet you at the station," he told her. "Do not say a word. No matter what they ask you, wait for the attorney to arrive."

Grayson shot Michael a "thanks a lot" look, but Michael either didn't notice or didn't care as he stood his ground. "Did you hear me, Melanie?" he pressed.

"I won't say a word," she murmured. Only then did Michael move out of the way.

Shannon stood next to him and watched Officer Brownley settle Melanie in the backseat of his SUV. She stared out the window, her eyes meeting Shannon's.

Shannon could barely stand to watch, but she had to give her friend an encouraging smile. The situation was horrible, truly horrible. Shannon had been through some difficult days in her life, but this one ranked near the top as one of the worst.

After the SUV departed, Shannon dropped onto the bench and stared into the distance as she tried to keep tears at bay.

"You're staying?" Michael asked.

"I promised Melanie I'd lock up when they're done."

"Do you want company?"

Shannon looked up to gauge his sincerity. "You'd stay?"

"If you want me to."

"That'd be nice, thank you." Shannon stood. "I should probably get inside and keep an eye on everyone like Melanie asked."

He held out his hand. "After you, then."

Inside, when she took a seat on the plaid sofa, Michael sat next to her. She snuck a sideways glance at him. He'd demonstrated his strength in so many ways, but his compassion in such a difficult time spoke volumes. She was truly glad he'd stayed.

He turned and caught her looking at him.

She smiled. "Thanks again for all you're doing to help," she said. "I'm sorry if I've been acting like a bit of a shrew lately. This whole situation is like a never-ending nightmare, and it's starting to wear on me."

"No need to apologize," he said. "And I'm happy to share whatever expertise I've gained over the years."

She sighed. "I never thought I'd need the expertise of a law-enforcement type."

He raised his brows. "Is that what 'type' I am? I didn't realize I was so easily categorized. Thanks for cluing me in," he teased.

"You know what I mean." Shannon felt herself blush and quickly changed the subject. "I wonder how Melanie is holding up."

"She appeared to be in shock. I only hope she takes my advice and doesn't say a word until the attorney gets there."

"It's not like she killed Edward and will confess to it," Shannon said. When she noticed Rachel glance over at them, she lowered her voice. "You believe that, don't you?"

"Yes, I do. But Miranda rights exist for a reason. Seemingly inconsequential things can be said, and when paired with evidence, those innocent remarks can lead to the conviction of innocent people."

"I can't imagine that happens often."

"More often than you'd think," Michael said.

Shannon couldn't believe what she was hearing. "Do you think Melanie might actually end up standing trial for murder?"

"It's possible." Michael's expression indicated he thought it was more than possible. "Part of it depends on how much investigating Grayson continues to do."

"Well, he has to keep looking for the real killer, doesn't he?"

"Not if he believes he already has the right person in custody."

"Then we have to do something!" Shannon clutched at his hand. "You said Grayson confides in you. Will you please go talk to him now?"

"Considering I warned Melanie not to say anything, I doubt he'll be willing to discuss the case with me," Michael said.

"But you can try, right?" Shannon urged, squeezing his hand. It wasn't until she saw him wince that she realized her nails were digging into his skin. Immediately, she dropped his hand. "Sorry."

An awkward moment of silence passed between them

before Michael finally spoke, "I can try talking to Grayson, but are you sure you want to be alone right now?"

She had no desire to be alone with her dreadful thoughts, but if Michael could help prove Melanie's innocence in any way, then he needed to go. "I'll be fine."

"How will you get home?"

Shannon had forgotten that she didn't have her truck. "I'll call the Purls, I'm sure one of them can come and get me."

"What about going to Ocean Tours?"

Shannon glanced at her watch. "They'll probably be closed by the time I'm finished here. It might have to wait until the morning."

"Don't go alone," he warned. "Call me before you go so I can accompany you."

"Sure," she said, realizing that for once, his drill sergeant tone didn't bother her one bit. "And you call me if you learn anything from Grayson."

"I will."

After he departed, a familiar chill enveloped Shannon. She peered out the window at the ocean waves rolling in. Even as she watched, the water churned harder and the waves turned even angrier. Another storm was on the horizon. She usually loved to watch the weather build into a powerful force, but at that moment, it only served as a reminder of her turmoil.

If Shannon had learned anything from the day's events, it was not to leave things undone. Melanie's arrest had proven there was no way to know what the future would bring. *I need to call Alec and my mother, and get everything out in the open.*

She dialed Alec first. *Please, God, let him answer, and let us work this out.*

"Hello, Mum." His deep voice sounded formal, but not mad.

Only an apology would smooth things over. "I'm sorry, Alec. I shouldn't have asked Coleen to come see you."

"No, you shouldn't have."

"You've been so withdrawn, I was worried about you," she explained. He said nothing in response, and Shannon feared he might never forgive her. "I know that's not an excuse, and I promise not to interfere that way again. I hope you can forgive me."

"Yes," Alec replied without hesitation.

One word. That's all he had for her when she wanted to know so much more. "I wish you could tell me what's wrong."

"I will." He sounded less frustrated with her, more tolerant of her need to be involved in the matter. "When I've sorted it out. OK?"

"Sure." She wanted desperately to be there to look into the deep green of his eyes and see that he was truly all right. But she couldn't—nor could she pursue the same line of thought without risking alienating him again. "Are you getting excited about coming to Oregon?"

"Sure," he said, but he didn't sound as if he meant it.

Was he quiet and unsettled because he'd changed his mind about moving to America? She couldn't handle that at all. "You do still want to move here, don't you?" she asked.

"Yes, of course." He sounded earnest, and Shannon tried to relax. "Look, I have a lot of homework to do. I'll talk to you later, OK, Mum? I love you."

"I love you too," she whispered, but she feared he'd hung up before he'd heard her. She'd hoped for a longer conversation, but at least he'd forgiven her for her mistake. And he'd said he loved her. That was a start. She had to give him space like Melanie had suggested, and everything would be all right.

Next she dialed Beth. After a few rings, the phone rolled to her mother's voice mail.

"It's Shannon," Shannon said after the beep. "I'm sorry I haven't gotten back to you sooner. I do want to meet for lunch and talk some more, but I need to concentrate on helping Melanie right now. I promise I'll call you as soon as this is resolved, and then we'll make a plan for a lunch date." She hung up, feeling more optimistic about her own life. And all it took was a few simple phone calls.

If only I could fix Melanie's life so easily.

16

Later that night, Shannon found herself driving through downtown Apple Grove, her truck sputtering at every stop sign. Thanks to Betty, she'd made it home from Melanie's safely. But the moment she'd stepped inside Paisley Manor, she realized she couldn't face the big, empty house alone. With hopes that Hank Gilliam had chosen to work late, she'd decided to head out to Ocean Tours instead. As she approached the downtown square and neared the police station, thoughts of Melanie confined in a cell like a hardened criminal filled her with sadness.

Rather than look at the station, she turned her head and kept her focus on the other side of the road, on the businesses she loved to frequent. Nearing The Flower Pot, she saw Elaina and Randy standing at the curb. As she drew closer, Elaina waved her arms, encouraging Shannon to stop. She didn't want to block the street, so she pulled into a parking space next to Randy's van, which boasted a large logo for Coastal Photos on its side.

She rolled down the window, the tight crank squeaking in protest. She noted dents and dings peppering the door of Randy's full-sized van, but the breathtaking ocean scene painted on the white body was in pristine condition.

Elaina, wearing jeans and a dark gray hoodie, hurried over to Shannon's truck. Her footsteps fell hard on the blacktop and echoed down the deserted street. Randy hung back, following at a slower pace.

Elaina planted her hands on the doorframe and gave Shannon a long searching look. "We saw Chief Grayson escort Melanie into the station—in handcuffs."

She seemed to be fishing for gossip, but Shannon wasn't surprised. The whole town would be buzzing about Melanie's arrest soon

Shannon remained silent, refusing to add to the gossip.

"Do they really have enough evidence to arrest her?" Elaina asked as Randy settled behind her, putting his hands on Elaina's shoulders.

"What do you think?" Shannon pulled a Michael, turning the question back at Elaina.

"They must have," Elaina replied, "or they wouldn't have arrested her—would they?"

Shannon responded with a shrug.

Elaina's eyebrows shot up. "I thought you two were friends. Don't you care about this?"

"Of course I do," Shannon replied. "I'm choosing not to gossip about my friend."

Elaina took a step back, edging closer to Randy. "I'm not gossiping, Shannon. Melanie is my friend too. She also works for me, in case you forgot. I'm trying to find out what's going on to see if I can do anything to help."

A pang of guilt jabbed Shannon. "I'm sorry. I guess I'm feeling a little defensive," she said.

"Why?" Elaina asked.

"Melanie asked me to help clear her name before something like this happened." Shannon pinched her thumb and index finger together and held them up. "And I'm this close to finding the real killer. In fact, I'm on my way to get the last bit of evidence I need."

"At this time of night?" Randy spoke for the first time. "Don't you think it's a little late?"

"It's never too late to help a friend."

"Is there anything we can do?" he asked. Elaina smiled up at him with blatant adoration.

"No, but thanks for offering," Shannon said.

"Let me give you my cell number in case you think of something we can do to help," Elaina offered.

Shannon doubted she would need Elaina's help, but she pulled out her phone and entered the numbers as Elaina rattled them off. "Got it," she said. "I should be going."

"Don't forget to call if you need us," Randy said, stepping back and drawing Elaina with him.

Shannon fired up the truck and revved the engine a few times to make sure it wasn't going to stall. Then she backed onto the street.

As she looked in her mirror, she saw Randy and Elaina return to his van. His arm was draped protectively over her shoulder, and she looked up at him, that adoring smile still plastered on her face. A pang of loneliness hit Shannon hard as the tires spun over damp roads.

She spotted the large Ocean Tours sign ahead. *Michael's going to be furious with me for coming here alone, but there's no time to waste.*

Even though she couldn't make out the lettering in the dark, she recognized the helicopter-shaped icon. The small hangar sat back from the road. She turned on her signal and whipped onto the rutted drive, slowing to ease over the deep potholes. A driveway in such a state of disrepair seemed odd for a business catering to tourists. *Has Hank been using his maintenance monies to pay off Edward?*

Lights shone at the base of the hangar, casting eerie reflections onto the corrugated steel. Shannon pulled up to the entrance and a security light flicked on. There were no other cars in the lot, but she figured Hank might be parked around back.

She turned off her pickup's engine, waiting as it coughed and sputtered before finally falling silent. Then she hopped out and jogged up to the main door. No lights shone through the window, and the door handle didn't budge when she tugged on it. She pounded on the door as hard as she could, but after a few minutes with no response, she decided to search for another door.

On the far end of the building, she located a door large enough to allow a helicopter to pass through. Next to it was a smaller door, also locked. She quickly circled around to the back. There were no lights, so she pulled out her cellphone and used it for a flashlight. She found a small parking area connected to the building, but it was devoid of any cars. Still, she walked to the back door and tried it too. *Locked.*

Shining her phone a few feet beyond the door, she saw a window. If it was unlocked, she may have finally found a way inside. She shoved her phone in her pocket and tugged on the rusted frame of the window. It groaned in protest but opened enough to allow her to climb inside.

Please don't let there be an alarm, she prayed as she landed on the floor with an ungraceful thud. She remained frozen in place for a few moments, listening. Other than the sound of howling wind, she heard nothing.

She dug out her phone again and held it up. It cast an eerie blue glow in the darkness. She could see an office in the far corner. A jumble of tools, machines, and a helicopter filled most of the open space around her. Careful not to step on anything, she inched across the room. It reeked of fuel. Hank obviously didn't bring visitors into the hangar.

Trying the office door, she found it unlocked. She stepped inside and paused for a moment, trying to get her bearings as she thought about what she was looking for. *Hank probably won't have a file sitting in the drawer labeled "FAA Violations." Maybe the best place to start will be to look for any files relating to Edward.*

Shannon flipped on the small desk lamp and pulled open a drawer. She found a section of personnel files—and one had Edward's name on it. When she opened his folder the first thing she saw was a termination notice.

She studied the document. He'd been fired eight months prior for not following the company's standard flight plan. She wondered if perhaps he'd used too much fuel. Or perhaps he'd flown too many hours, and that violated the FAA rules. Or maybe it had something to do with a specific customer.

All good things to check.

As she started to put the folder back, several aerial photos of the coast slid out. She flipped through them and noticed they'd been shot at the exact same spot on the coast that she'd seen in Edward's Internet searches, the location with pollution issues.

She quickly snapped pictures of them with the camera on her cellphone and replaced the folder.

Hoping the identity of the customer who'd taken the flight would be of help, she rolled back to the desk to look for a booking schedule. She dug through piles until she located a grungy white binder with "Calendar" written on the front in black marker. Just as she flipped open the cover, a loud clanging sound cut through the silence of the hangar.

I'm not alone.

Shannon bolted from the chair and snapped off the light. Blinded by the sudden darkness, she stared out the door, straining to see. A few seconds later, she heard what sounded like a metal tool clanging against the concrete floor on the other side of the hangar.

Please let it be a nosy cat and not a deranged killer.

Fear gripped her. She had to get out of the office before she got trapped. She slid along the wall, feeling the rough texture with her fingers.

Another sound reached her ears. Footsteps, whisper soft, but purposeful and drawing nearer. Her pulse pounded in her neck. She tried to move faster, but her feet felt like they were made of concrete.

Another loud clang rang out, this one even closer. She froze. The moon broke free of the heavy clouds and shone through a large window at the top of the hangar. The misty beam of light illuminated the room in a cloudy haze. She could now make out her surroundings. At least enough to see if anything blocked her escape.

And enough for the intruder to see me.

Her heart clutched, and her steps faltered. A whispering

noise made her spin around. She focused on the spot where she'd heard the sound and saw the unmistakable outline of a man in the shadows.

Shannon swallowed hard against her bone-dry throat. The man crept closer, stealthy and agile. She couldn't identify him in the low light. But if she hid, she might have the opportunity to identify him.

At what cost? her mind screamed. *Your own life, if he finds you?*

One thing was certain: she couldn't continue to stand there like a simpleton. She had to decide—get out or hide. *I'll be of no help to Melanie if I don't make it out of this hangar alive. I have to get out of here!* Her decision made, she eased along the wall, heading for the door. Judging by the direction of the soft thuds of the man's footfalls, he was slowly making his way to the office.

Shannon unlocked the back door of the hangar and cringed as the click echoed through the cavernous space like a gunshot. Fearing she'd given away her location, she gave up trying to be stealthy and jerked the door open. She ran hard and fast, her breath hitching as she moved. As she charged around the corner of the hangar, she and nearly slammed into a Coastal Photos van parked next to the building.

Shannon stared at the vehicle in shock, gasping for air.

Is Elaina's boyfriend involved in this? Could he be the man inside? He was of the same build and size as the man she'd seen. But what could Randy possibly have to do with Edward?

Elaina. Shannon's mind reeled as it dawned on her that Elaina might actually be the killer. As owner of The Flower

Pot, she'd certainly know about oleander. Perhaps she was in the van right now, waiting for her accomplice to come out.

Shannon eased closer to the vehicle and peered in the passenger window, but the front seats were empty. Then she moved to the back windows and looked in. It was too dark to see inside, but she didn't think Elaina would be hiding out in the back of the van.

The sound of metal groaning behind her grabbed Shannon's attention.

The hangar door. He's coming for me. She took off, running as fast as she could, digging in her pocket for her keys. As she rounded the corner of the building, her blue pickup came into view. She'd never been so glad to see Old Blue.

Shannon wrenched open the door, jumped in, and cranked the engine. It faltered, as usual.

She cranked it again and it sputtered.

"Come on, start!" She turned the key one more time and held her breath, waiting for the engine to catch.

It finally rumbled into a smooth purr. She quickly slammed the gearshift into first and then floored the gas pedal. The truck lurched forward, jerking and shaking as it went. She kept her focus ahead until she was certain the truck wouldn't stall. Then she dared to glance back in the big side mirror.

Randy stood in the middle of the empty lot, watching her go. He looked otherworldly as the misty night closed around him.

Shannon shivered. Had she set her own death sentence by letting him see her? Only time would tell.

— 17 —

Shannon pushed the speed limit as she approached downtown Apple Grove. How surreal it all felt. The picturesque small town that had captivated her heart lay before her, while a man who might be a killer followed behind.

Not that she'd seen his van in her rearview mirror. If he *was* following her, he wasn't getting close enough to let her see him. But he could still be there. Randy had to know she'd seen his vehicle. But would he really try to harm her at this point? If he *had* murdered Edward, he'd meticulously planned out every detail of the killing so he wouldn't be implicated.

Surely he wouldn't put all of that at risk just because he saw me at the hangar! Shannon thought—and hoped.

Then again, Randy might have had a legitimate reason for being at the hangar. Maybe he worked with Hank at Ocean Tours. Perhaps Hank provided the transportation for Randy to take aerial photos. But that still didn't explain Randy skulking through the building in the dark.

Shannon slowed as she approached the four-way stop in the middle of town. The lights were still on at The Flower Pot; which meant Elaina was working late. Shannon eased the truck forward slowly as she peered into the shop. Elaina sat behind the counter. It looked like she was doing paperwork.

Shannon braked to a stop. *Should I confront her?*

She had no proof that either Randy or Elaina was involved in Edward's death. And if they were, confronting Elaina would only tip them off that she was on to them. She had to discover their connection to Edward before she said anything.

I'll look through the copies of Edward's records again to see if he had any association with Randy or Elaina.

Shannon put the truck into gear and set off slowly, careful not to alert Elaina to her presence. During the short drive home, she kept a watch in her rearview mirror for any sign of Randy. But the road behind her was empty. Surely if he were the killer, he would have tailed her.

She parked in front of the house and ran up the steps. Inside, she shivered at the darkened foyer and switched on every light. *I will be so glad when Deborah returns.*

After making sure the front door was locked behind her, she hurried to her study and settled in front of the small desk behind her computer. She plugged her phone into her computer and started to upload the pictures she'd taken at the hangar. As they transferred, she searched the listing of websites Edward had visited until she located the links for the stories about coastal pollution.

The county had been cited several times for high levels of contaminants where the river ran through the county and emptied into the ocean. Shannon clicked on the uploaded photos and compared them to the online story.

Unique rock formations showed it to be the exact same location as in the article.

Had Edward caught someone polluting the river as she'd suspected? Maybe the culprit was Coastal Photos, not Ocean Tours. She searched for Coastal Photos' address and plugged it into an online map site. The company head-quarters was located on the river.

Excitement starting to build, Shannon read the article in more detail. It gave no information about the type of pollutants found in the river, but if she could prove the contaminants contained chemicals used in photo processing, that could help link Randy to the pollution and a potential blackmailing scheme by Edward.

A quick search, however, located no reports.

Michael. He might have a contact at the county who could get the contaminant report quickly. Smiling, she grabbed her cellphone and dialed, then settled back to wait for him to answer.

The floorboard creaked behind her.

Shannon turned just as a muscular arm shot around her chest, pinning her against the chair. A scream tore from her throat an instant before a large hand clamped over her mouth. She struggled to free herself, and he tightened his hold, both arms clamping her in place.

"Hang up," the man whispered against her hair.

She instinctively recoiled, trying to jerk away, but he held firm. She screamed against his hand.

"I said hang it up." His fingers pressed down hard on her mouth.

She ceased struggling and prayed he wouldn't risk taking either arm off her to knock the phone from her hand. Michael had likely answered by now, and if she had any hope of rescue, she needed to keep him on the line. Thinking fast, she decided to lower the volume all the way and pretend to hang up. That way Michael could listen in on the call, but the intruder wouldn't hear Michael if he spoke.

She depressed her thumb on the volume button.

"Nice try, sweetheart," he whispered. "Now hang it up if you don't want me to snap your neck right now."

Shannon knew in her gut that the man meant to kill her regardless, so she took one last chance. Pretending to press her finger on the "End Call" button, she laid it facedown on the desk, praying he wouldn't turn it over.

"Good," he purred. "Now I'm going to take my hand off your mouth. If you scream, I'll kill you. Understand?"

She tried to nod. He released her mouth and wrapped a thick rope around her right wrist, relaxing his hold on her ever so slightly. Could she slip away from him? It might be her only opportunity. *I have to try.*

She jumped up and jerked her hand.

He yanked her back down with the rope and then twisted her wrist painfully.

She cried out, but he didn't release his hold.

"Foolish woman. Give me your other hand, or I'll twist until I hear something break."

Eyes stinging with pain, she complied.

He clamped her hands together, and she felt the coarse rope twine around both wrists. He tugged hard, causing the rope to bite into her tender skin. She stifled another cry of pain and sat rigidly, refusing to give him the satisfaction of knowing how much he was hurting her.

"You couldn't leave this alone, could you?" After the final tug of a solid knot, the man came around the front of the chair and looked down on her.

Shannon glared up—at Randy. "You killed Edward, didn't you?"

"I did." His lips tipped in a self-satisfied smile. "And you're next."

Her heart thumped hard against her chest, but she fought for calm. "You actually think you can get away with murder twice?"

"Yes, because no one will think you were murdered. You're going to have a nice little accident at the hangar," he sneered. "Hank will be so shocked when he arrives at work in the morning to find that you had a fatal accident while snooping around his property."

Shannon's heart plummeted. Randy was going to kill her and get away with it—just as he'd done with Edward. Her only chance for survival was to try and stall him, and hope Michael arrived to intervene before it was too late.

Slim chance. But I have to try.

"I don't think you'll get away with Ed's murder," Shannon said, fixing him with a cool gaze to hide her inner turmoil. "It's obvious why you killed him: He caught you dumping chemicals."

A look of surprise lit Randy's face. "Well, aren't you the clever one. Fortunately, Grayson's not quite as bright. You're right; Ed spotted me on one of his trips. He snapped a few pictures, and then he blackmailed me."

"Why would you let him blackmail you? You're not in any of the photos."

"You mean these?" He jerked a thumb toward her monitor, and she nodded. "I've already found and destroyed all the photos I was in. These won't convict me of anything."

"Then why were they in Edward's personnel file?" Shannon challenged.

"Ed used them to give Hank a reason for veering off the course that day. He told Hank he was going to sell the pictures to a newspaper reporter who was doing a story on the pollution." Randy shook his head. "Ed didn't count on Hank getting mad at him for freelancing while he was on Hank's payroll. Hank fired him that very day. Not like it mattered. I was paying him enough to live on. Until I got tired of paying." He lips curled in a proud smirk. "I did a great job of framing Melanie, didn't I?"

"Not really. I was only moments away from figuring out you were behind this. Just as Grayson will," Shannon said.

Randy's expression darkened. "Liar! You don't have any evidence to pin the murder on me."

Shannon wanted to offer a smart retort, but it would only anger him further—and that wouldn't bode well for staying alive.

"I've had enough of you. Let's get going," Randy said.

"Wait!" she blurted, desperate to keep him talking. "You never mentioned where you killed him. Was it Melanie's house?"

"Bit of genius to do it there, don't you think?"

Swallowing hard, Shannon tried to appear impressed. "Very clever. How did you get into her house?'

"It was easy. Ed never kept his mouth shut—shot it off whenever the guys got together."

"So you were friends with Ed before he started blackmailing you?" she asked. *Come on, Michael. You have to know something is wrong.*

"Friends?" Randy paused as if thinking. "Not really. We hung out at the same bar. That's where I heard him say he still had a key to Melanie's house. He was biding his time until he figured out how to use it to get back at her for snagging the house in the divorce settlement."

"So you took his key to steal the needle and frame Melanie," Shannon said, feeling a bead of sweat run down her forehead.

"Indeed I did. But I didn't just take the needle. I dragged him into her house before he died and plunged it into the jerk's neck right there in the dining room." He laughed again. "It was amazing. There I was, right in her house, and she didn't have a clue. I tied him up using her yarn and then made a few searches on her computer. I cleaned up most of the blood afterward—as any guilty ex-spouse would do, careful to leave just enough behind to incriminate Melanie."

"Why not leave him there for her to find?"

"What fun would that be?" He rubbed his hand over his chin. "Now, I'd love to stay and chat, but we really must be going."

Shannon panicked. "But I have to know, why did you choose my craft store garden as the burial site?"

Randy mocked an apologetic look. "Sorry if I hurt your feelings. It wasn't anything against you. Elaina had been going on and on about the new addition and the dedication ceremony. It seemed like a fitting way to have his body discovered."

"You're sick," Shannon spat, unable to act civil to the monster for another second.

His eyes narrowed. "Probably not a good idea to insult the person who has you tied up."

"What difference does it make? You're going to kill me anyway."

Randy shrugged. "Right you are. Let's get on with it." He jerked her up by the rope, burning her wrists painfully in the process.

"An ainm an àigh!" she exclaimed.

"I don't know what you just said, but I didn't like your tone. We're taking your truck." He lifted the keys from the desktop and dangled them in front of her face. "Is your truck key on here?"

"No."

"I'll take that as a yes." He shoved the keys in his pocket and then jerked her forward by the rope. She stumbled, and as her hands flew up to right herself, he let go. She tumbled to the floor, pain biting into her knees. He stared down at her, laughing, low and sinister.

How did I ever think he was a nice man?

Randy tugged her to her feet again and shoved her out onto the porch.

She scanned the driveway and grounds. Darkness shrouded the usually beautiful and tranquil property. She searched for any sign of Michael, but found none. Her phone trick hadn't worked.

Dread coiled in her stomach like a viper. No one was coming to help her. She was on her own.

— 18 —

Shannon paused on the porch at the top of the curving stairs and tried to calm herself with a deep breath. She looked back longingly at Paisley Manor. *Will tonight be the last time I see my grandmother's beloved home?*

Randy yanked on the rope and jerked her forward. Anger at his manhandling rose up, and she knew then and there that she would not let him kill her without a fight. She'd find a way to get out of his clutches.

He pulled open the passenger door to her pickup. "Get in," he growled.

As she climbed in, she prayed that the truck wouldn't start, or that Randy wouldn't be able to handle a stick shift. Looking around for something she could use to free herself, she spotted her knitting basket on the floor, and an idea hit her. When he closed the door, she would grab her scissors and hide them beneath her legs. Then, when the time presented itself, she'd use them to wound him and make her escape.

She settled onto the worn seat and waited until he slammed the door. As he hurried around the front of the truck, she clumsily pawed through the basket, struggling against the painful rope that bound her wrists. Finally, she found her scissors and triumphantly pulled them free.

Feeling a little giddy from the stress of the situation,

she nearly broke out into nervous laughter. If anyone had told her that someday her yarn-clipping scissors would save her life, she'd have thought them mad. But it was fitting— stabbing the man who'd stabbed Edward.

Randy opened the driver's side door just as she slid the scissors in place beneath her leg and leaned back against the seat. She tried not to look guilty, turning her face away from him to stare out the window.

He climbed in and pulled the door closed. The sound of metal scraping on hinges sent her nerves firing. "This is such a sweet ride," he said. "Be nice if I could keep it. I mean, it's not like you'll be needing it anymore."

Please don't let it start, she prayed.

"You sure are quiet all of a sudden," Randy said as he leaned across her to press the door lock. "Wouldn't want you bailing on me at a stop sign."

Shannon flattened herself against the back of the seat as he moved across her so he wouldn't touch her. When he cranked the engine, it started on the first try, purring like a contented cat.

Och! Shannon clenched her fist. *Two-timing old truck!*

"For what it's worth, I am sorry I have to do this," Randy said, once they were on the road. "Elaina thinks the world of you, and I know she'll freak out when she hears about your accident."

I should try to keep him talking. "Was she in on Ed's death?"

"Elaina?" He shook his head. "No. Her only part in all of it was to answer a few questions about poisonous plants. She had no idea what I planned to do with the information."

"And you don't think once the oleander poisoning

becomes public knowledge that she'll remember your conversation and figure out you killed him?"

"Please," Randy chuckled. "Did you see the way she looks at me? There's no way she'd ever think I did anything wrong. The woman worships the ground I walk on."

Shannon felt sick to her stomach—not only for herself, but for poor Elaina who was apparently infatuated with a deranged lunatic. "She's going to be devastated when your part in Ed's murder and my attempted murder comes out," she said.

"You sound awful confident you're going to get away and turn me in." Randy slowed to a stop at a four-way intersection and studied her, his expression turning paranoid. "You hiding something from me?"

"What could I possibly be hiding?" Shannon asked. She forced herself not to look away and emptied her brain of any subterfuge she had planned. Lying was not her forté.

"Good question." Seeming satisfied, Randy pressed on the gas, and the truck started moving again.

Shannon eased out a breath. She turned away and looked out the window. They passed the familiar businesses on Main Street, now closed up for the night. She focused on her craft market, then The Flower Pot, the Pink Sprinkles Bakery, and Ultimutt Grooming. Her eyes lingered the longest on Stone & McCrary in hopes that Michael would be there and spot her. But his business was dark like all the others.

I will handle this on my own. Melanie needed her to prevail. And the twins needed her to prevail. Failure to outsmart Randy simply wasn't an option.

They didn't pass a single car before arriving at Ocean Tours, located on the edge of town. Randy swung into the lot and pulled around to the side where Shannon had climbed through the open window earlier in the night. It seemed like that had happened weeks ago, but it had only been a few hours. As he rolled to a stop, she settled her hands in her lap, waiting for the right moment to execute her plan.

She started to reach for the scissors and he jerked his face toward her. Immediately, she froze, feeling her hope begin to slip away.

He knows about the scissors.

With a wicked gleam in his eye, Randy leaned in close to her and stretched his arm across her again to unlock the door. "This is it, cupcake," he said.

You're right about that. This is it—for you.

As he slid back to his side of the truck, Shannon pretended to shiver and hunched over. She inched the scissors forward until she could grip them firmly.

Randy reached for the keys. She turned, and with all her might, she plunged the scissors into his thigh. The keys flew from his fingers as he roared like a wounded lion. She jerked the scissors out, and blood gushed from the wound.

Like a mad man, he frantically pressed his hand on the injury, screaming in rage, "You'll pay for this!"

Shannon didn't waste time with a response. She kicked her door open, but with her hands bound, she lost her balance and tumbled onto the pavement, dropping the scissors. The asphalt bit into her already bruised knees, but she didn't care. She could taste freedom.

She pushed to her feet and ran blindly though the dark,

all thoughts but escaping gone from her mind. Her breath hitched and her side ached, but she kept going.

Randy's footfalls pounded up the driveway behind her, a solid thump, thump, thump echoing through the chilly night air.

Shannon glanced back and saw him gaining ground, moving surprisingly fast for a man with an injured leg. She kicked into high gear again, but could still hear him closing in on her. His legs were far longer than hers. Panic overtook her as she realized that she couldn't outrun him. Not with her hands bound together. *I have to hide.*

Veering off the drive, she ducked into a thick stand of tall pines. She had to slow down to keep from tripping over roots. Twigs snapped under her feet as she pushed through the rough branches.

Moments later, Randy crashed into the brush behind her, but he didn't slow down. He sounded as if he were flying over the rough terrain, moving fast, way too fast.

Instinctively, Shannon tried to speed up again, but her legs screamed with fatigue, and instead, her body slowed. She knew she couldn't keep up the burning pace much longer, but she also knew that if she slowed down even a fraction more, he would kill her—and she didn't want to die.

— 19 —

Shannon heard a sudden rush of noise behind her. The sound of crashing branches and breaking twigs came from a different direction. Suddenly, Randy's footfalls stopped, and she heard thrashing on the ground.

Slowing slightly, she risked a quick peek behind her. She saw Randy on the ground, but he wasn't alone. Another man wrestled with him.

Am I hallucinating? Could it really be Michael?

Joy took hold, but she forced down her excitement in case she truly was losing her mind under the stress of it all. She came to a full stop and turned, fighting the urge to run back and identify the other man. But she couldn't risk it. Instead she collapsed behind a tree and listened. Occasional grunts sounded from the men until the tussling stopped.

"Give it up, Parson," Michael's voice rang out. "The police are on their way."

As if Michael had summoned the police simply by speaking about them, sirens split the quiet, sending Shannon's heart soaring to the moon. Thank goodness, they were coming. They were really coming. She never thought she'd be so glad to see Grayson. She pushed herself to her feet and stepped out from behind the tree. On rubbery legs, she made her way to Michael.

He looked up at her, but it was too dark to get a read

on his expression. "Are you all right?" he asked, pushing Randy's face into a bed of pine needles.

"I'm fine," she said, though her legs threatened to give out at any moment.

The sirens grew louder and blue lights filtered through the fog, lighting the skies as the police vehicles raced into the parking lot.

"We'll wait here for Grayson," Michael announced, sounding a bit winded.

Shannon looked at the forest around them. "How will he find us out here?"

"He's a cop. He'll find us."

It all hit her then. The stress came pouring out in the form of tears, and her legs couldn't hold her upright. She sank to the ground and smiled as she cried. She was safe, *really* safe. And as a bonus, she'd found the real killer. *Melanie will go free.*

"Are you hurt?" Michael asked, his concern obvious.

"No," she choked out. "I was so afraid. I didn't think you'd heard my conversation with Randy."

"What conversation?" Randy asked, his voice muffled.

"When you told me to disconnect my phone, I didn't. I left the speaker on and apparently Michael was able to hear our conversation." She waited for Randy to respond, but he didn't say a word.

"I heard your whole confession, Parson," Michael added. "Chief Grayson was most interested when I told him about it."

"It's all hearsay," Randy protested as he tried to shift, but Michael jerked his arm higher eliciting a groan.

"Keep telling yourself that. At a minimum, you're going away for kidnapping and attempted murder."

Shannon heard the sirens cut out, then loud footsteps pounding on the driveway. A few moments of silence were followed by the rustling of brush.

"We're back here!" Michael called out. "Grayson? You copy?"

"Roger," Grayson's voice rang out loud and strong. "You got Parson?"

"Yes."

"What about Shannon?" The chief demanded.

"She's fine."

Fine was such a strong word for how she was feeling. But she *would* be fine once Grayson hauled Randy off and Melanie was released. Shannon leaned back against rough tree bark and pulled her legs up to her chest. Before long, she spotted a light dancing in the distance. It grew larger as the sound of crunching leaves got stronger.

Grayson burst through the scrub, looking confident and sure, even though he'd put the wrong person in jail. He pulled handcuffs from his belt and held them out to Michael. "You want to do the honors?"

"A bit unorthodox, but I'm more than happy to do it," Michael replied and took the cuffs. Grayson shone the light on Randy's hands, and Michael snapped the metal bands around his wrists.

Grayson handed the flashlight to Michael and he climbed off Randy. With a yank of the cuffs, Grayson jerked Randy to his feet.

Randy moaned. "Careful of my leg!"

Michael and the other officer shone their lights on Randy's leg. His jeans were soaked in blood, even though he'd tied the scarf from Shannon's knitting basket around his leg.

"What happened, Parson? You fall and get a boo-boo?" Grayson asked.

Randy scowled at Shannon. "She stabbed me with scissors." He sounded so insulted that Shannon felt the urge to laugh at the absurdness of it.

"Another stabbing?" Grayson looked at Shannon with surprise. "That's twice since you've come to town. We ought to require a permit to buy those crafty supplies you ladies like so much."

"But it's a good thing she had it," Michael said, fixing Grayson with a stern look.

"True," Grayson admitted. "And it serves you right, Parson." He pushed Randy up against a tree and searched him as he read him his rights.

When he finished, the chief hauled Randy away from the tree by the cuffs, much the way Randy had jerked Shannon around with the rope. "Let's go, Parson."

"Grayson," Shannon called out, "you'll release Melanie immediately, right?"

"As soon as I get this guy processed."

"Can I come to the station and wait?" she asked.

"Sure."

Michael turned to her. "Can I help you up?"

Shannon held out her hands, still bound with the irritating rope. "It would be more helpful if you could get this off me."

He shone his light on her hands and muttered something under his breath. He knelt in front of her and tucked the flashlight under his arm. Then, he dug out a pocketknife and tenderly took her wrists in his hands.

She glanced at the knife he held. "Always prepared. You must've been a boy scout," she mused, feeling a little lightheaded.

"A soldier, actually. U.S. Army."

"Ah, that explains why you order others about so easily—and by 'others', I mean me."

He looked up, but there was no humor in his eyes. "I'm sorry this happened to you, Shannon. I wish I'd gotten to you sooner."

"Hey," she said, "you don't need to apologize. You came through for me, and that's all that matters. Once again, you've saved my life. At this rate, I'm not sure how I'll ever be able to dig myself out of your debt."

"You're not in my debt." He sawed at the rope, and she tried not to wince as it bit into already raw flesh. When the cord gave way and dropped to the ground, she started to pull free. But Michael turned her hands over and examined her wrists, hissing out a breath. "They dispatched an ambulance, too, so we'll have them look at this."

She brushed him away. "There's no need. I'll be fine."

He fixed a firm stare on her, and she shivered under the dark intensity of his eyes. He held out his hand. "Come with me."

"Yes sir." She slipped her chilled fingers into the warmth of his and rose to her feet. She wobbled, but he steadied her with a hand under her elbow.

"Are you sure you're OK to walk?" he asked.

An image of him scooping her up into his arms and carrying her to the driveway popped into her mind and made her blush. *What am I, the helpless heroine in a romance novel?*

"I got back here on my own. I can get out on my own." She pulled her hand free of his grasp and set off in what she hoped was the right direction.

He came up beside her, walking a little too close for her comfort.

"If we stay close together, we'll both benefit from the light," he said. He held the flashlight out so that the beam danced on the ground ahead of them.

Once on the driveway, he steered her toward the ambulance with a gentle hand on her back. She wanted to hop into her truck and take off for the police station, but she knew he'd argue, and that would take more time than letting the paramedic apply a few bandages.

They approached the medic, a cute blonde who looked to be in her early 30s.

"Hey, Michael." She smiled up at him, ignoring Shannon completely.

"Terrie, can you look at Shannon's wrists?" He urged Shannon closer.

Shannon held out her arms. In the light spilling from the ambulance, she could see how raw and torn her flesh was. No wonder the pain was so intense. Feeling queasy, she looked away. She could handle bandaging her kids—anyone else, really—but when it came to looking at her own wounds, she always got squeamish.

"Rope burns, huh?" Terrie said. "Have a seat on the bumper, and I'll take a closer look."

Shannon sat, thankful to be off her still-rubbery legs. Terrie got out a pair of tweezers, some salve, and gauze bandages. She sat next to Shannon and took one of her wrists in capable hands. "There're some fibers in here that I need to get out. It might sting a little."

Shannon looked up, and her eyes must have given away her anxiety because Michael smiled and squatted next to her.

"I didn't know you were such a baby," he teased. "I thought Scottish women were more ... hardy."

"I can't believe you would poke fun at my heritage during a time like this," she said, trying not to smile. "And yes, this Scottish woman gets squeamish at the sight of her own blood."

"Look on the bright side," Terrie said. "You're not nearly as bad off as the dude with a hole in his leg."

"You took care of him?" Shannon asked.

"As much as I could." Terrie tugged on Shannon's skin, making her wince. "Sorry. A doctor will have to take a look at that guy's leg to make sure there isn't any muscle damage."

Muscle damage. Shannon frowned, feeling guilty. Then she was instantly mad at herself for having even an ounce of compassion for the man who had just tried to kill her.

"Hey." Michael squeezed her hand. "I know that look. Don't go there. You have nothing to feel guilty about."

"Wait a second." Terrie's head popped up. "You're the one who stabbed him?"

"I'm the one."

"Nice job." Terrie winked at her and went back to work.

Will everyone in town react that way? Or will people whisper and keep their distance? Only time would tell.

"Once we're done here," Michael said, drawing her attention again, "I'll take you to the station to get Melanie."

"I can drive," she insisted, pulling her hand from his so Terrie could treat her other wrist.

"Actually," he said, his tone hinting at bad news, "your truck is now part of a crime scene, so it will have to stay here until Grayson's team finishes processing it."

She shifted her focus to her grandmother's truck and felt sick. The wonderful old piece of history now had blood in it. She didn't much like driving the old beater, and the moody old thing clearly felt zero loyalty to her, but she loved having something of her grandparent's in her life. Now the truck would forever be tainted by memories of Randy.

"You know that truck belonged to my grandmother—and to my grandfather before that," she said. "It's bad enough there's blood in it, but now a forensics team is going to add powders and sprays to the mess?"

"Maybe not," he said. "Besides, you can have the interior professionally cleaned."

Shannon frowned. "Unfortunately, the memory of Randy plotting to kill me will still be there."

Michael's eyes suddenly flooded with pain. "I understand how you feel. I had a similar problem a long time ago, when I lost someone very close to me."

His wife. Shannon recalled Deborah telling her and Coleen how a drug lord had shot Michael's wife in retaliation for a drug bust when he was a police officer in Portland. But since Michael had never told her about it himself, Shannon wasn't exactly sure how to respond.

"I'm so sorry," Shannon whispered.

Even Terrie stopped working and looked at him.

He blinked and stood up, seeming to shake off his melancholy. "I'll go see if Grayson is OK with you leaving when Terrie finishes."

Shannon looked up at him. "Why wouldn't he be?"

"He'll need an official statement from you. I'm not sure if he wants to do it here or at the station." Michael took off so fast, Shannon felt certain he was fleeing.

She watched him stride away.

"He's really something, isn't he?" Terrie asked as she grabbed a tube of ointment. "So mysterious. Makes you want to figure out what makes him tick. Doesn't hurt that he's gorgeous either ...."

Terrie babbled on as she wound a bandage around Shannon's wrist, but Shannon kept her focus on Michael. Terrie was right. Her first instinct was to chase after him and try to get him to open up more, at least finish sharing his story. But after everything she'd just been through, she knew she wasn't up to such an insurmountable task.

20

"**A**re you sure you don't mind if I use your phone to call the twins?" Shannon asked Michael from the passenger's seat of his car.

"Not at all."

She settled into the soft leather and dialed Lara, enjoying the warmth from the heated seats. She could get used to such luxury in a car. It sure beat fighting with a temperamental old truck.

"Mum." Lara answered on the first ring. "Is something wrong?'

"No, everything's fine. I needed to hear your voice, that's all."

"Mum ..." Lara let out an impatient sigh. "I miss you too, but it's only a few weeks until I see you."

"I know, and I won't keep you. I just wanted to tell you that I love you, sweetie."

"I love you too," Lara answered, though her voice said she was still confused by the call.

"I'll talk to you soon." Shannon disconnected and dialed Alec's cell. It rang and rang and rang until she finally got his voice mail.

"No," she said. "Not this time."

She dialed again.

"Mum," he answered sounding breathless.

"You sound out of breath. Are you OK?"

"Fine. I was coming back from the loo and heard my phone ringing, so I ran the rest of the way." He paused. "Hey, why're you calling so early, anyway?"

"I need to say I'm sorry again about sending Coleen to check up on you. I respect you and trust you, Alec. You're a man now, and I promise to give you space whenever you need it."

For a long moment, she got nothing but silence. Then, finally, he said, "Thanks. I'd hoped not to have to tell you this." He paused, and Shannon dreaded hearing what he would say next. "But my grades aren't as good as I'm sure you're expecting."

Grades! Was all of his melodrama about grades? "Are you finding the courses too difficult?"

"No, no, it's not that. You see ... I met this girl, and I've ... well, I've kind've been slacking off. Then everything seemed to be due at once."

She laughed long and hearty.

"What's that supposed to mean, Mum? Are you *laughing* at me?"

"No, of course not. I know you may not think this, but I was your age once, and I know what it's like to fall in love for the first time."

"I never said it was love." He sounded completely grossed out by the turn the conversation had taken.

"OK, fine," she said. "I know what it's like to ditch my classes and spend time with someone I care about."

"You ditched classes?" he said, his voice incredulous.

"Occasionally." She laughed. "Is this serious? With the girl, I mean."

"Maybe, but it really doesn't matter since I won't be living here for much longer."

Shannon's stomach clenched. "You're not thinking of staying there, are you?"

"No, but I may want to visit."

She smiled. "Then you'll have to give me a call at a decent time of day, and we'll work all of this out."

"Thanks, Mum, for being so understanding about everything."

"I love you, Son."

"I love you too."

Shannon hung up, her heart bursting with joy. "One more quick call," she said to Michael. Then dialed her mother.

"Hello," Beth answered, sounding sleepy.

"It's Shannon. I hope I'm not calling too late."

"No. I'm so glad you called."

"I promised I would when everything worked out for Melanie."

"And has it?"

"Yes." Shannon's heart warmed with the thought. "I'll tell you all about it at lunch tomorrow. That is, if you're free?"

"Absolutely," Beth answered without hesitation.

"I don't want us to be distracted during our talk, so let's not meet in Apple Grove."

"We can go to my favorite seafood place, then." Beth named a popular restaurant in Astoria. "Would one o'clock work for you?"

"Sounds perfect. I'll see you then." Shannon disconnected, and a contented sigh slipped out as she settled into the warm leather seat. All was right with the world again. Well, almost all. After Melanie's release, things would be perfect.

* * *

Shannon sat on the cold metal chair in an interrogation room at the Apple Grove Police Station. She'd assumed Melanie would be waiting to go home when she arrived. But, as usual, the chief had other plans.

He insisted on taking Shannon's statement before releasing Melanie. And that meant question after question, each little detail of her time with Randy analyzed and scrutinized. All she could think about as they'd hashed it all out was that Melanie had been forced to sit in the very same room and endure questioning about a crime she didn't commit. Only Grayson had no doubt been harsher with her.

Finally the chief slapped a piece of paper on the table in front of her. "Read this, and if it's all correct, sign at the bottom."

Shannon picked up the page and read the typed account of her kidnapping and attempted murder. Every word she read brought back the incident, and she wondered how long it would take to forget the whole ordeal.

Will I ever forget?

She shook off her melancholy and scribbled her name across the bottom. "Can I take Melanie home now?" she asked.

"Head back to the reception area, and I'll have her brought out to you."

Shannon made no move to leave, staring at Grayson

expectantly—waiting for an apology for not listening to her about Melanie's innocence.

He seemed to wilt a little under her observation. "I was just doing my job, Shannon. And I'd arrest her again tomorrow if the evidence pointed in the same direction," he said.

Shannon started to argue with him, but then she remembered what Michael had told her about Grayson following the law. Michael was right. She wanted to live in a town where the chief of police did his job, even if it wasn't pleasant for him.

Without a word, she headed out the door and down the very sterile hallway. In the foyer, she found Michael pacing.

"Did everything go OK?" he asked.

"It went fine. Grayson is going to have someone bring Melanie up here."

"I hope you won't let this experience make you doubt the police," he said. "It's important that you understand Grayson didn't do anything wrong."

She opened her mouth to say she'd already reached that conclusion, but he held up his hand and continued. "A police officer has to follow the facts as they're presented and make a case based on that. Sometimes it leads them to the wrong conclusion, but most often, if they have enough evidence to obtain an arrest warrant, then they've made a good case."

"Spoken like a true cop," she teased, trying to lighten the mood. "How long has it been since you left the force?"

"A little over ten years."

"If you miss it so much, why did you leave?" Shannon asked, watching the muscles in his jaw clench as he seemed to war over a decision.

"I mentioned earlier that someone close to me was murdered." Michael ran fingers through his thick hair. "It happened because of my job—it was my wife."

"And you blame yourself."

Pain darkened his blue eyes, turning them almost black. "There's no one else to blame."

Before she could probe further, the door opened, and Melanie emerged carrying a manila envelope. Shannon assumed it held her belongings taken at booking. Melanie's face was haggard, her hair a mess, and her clothes wrinkled.

But she was free.

Melanie surveyed the room, and when she spotted Shannon, all worry drained from her face. "Shannon!"

Shannon rushed over to her. "I'm sorry it took me so long to get you out of here," she said.

"Are you kidding?" Melanie grinned. "If it wasn't for you, they would have locked me up and thrown away the key."

"You ready to get out of this place?" Shannon asked.

Melanie took one last look around the room and grimaced. "Absolutely."

"Michael will drive us. You're spending the night with me, no arguments." Unable to wait any longer; Shannon swept Melanie into a big hug.

"Michael, huh?" Melanie whispered as she hugged Shannon tightly.

"Yes." Shannon looked over Melanie's shoulder and caught his eye. He smiled at her as his icy-blue eyes met hers. "He's been such a good friend to me this past week."

"Well, we all need good *friends*," Melanie said. "And I'm so thankful I have *you* for a friend."

"Right back at you."

They pulled apart.

Melanie's eyes widened. "Hey, do you still have any of your delicious cheesecake left?" she asked. "I've passed my time in this place fantasizing about it—I think it's what kept me going."

Shannon laughed. "Are you kidding? I have a whole freezer full. Come on. We'll call the other Purls on the way to my house. We have much to celebrate."

Big Time Vest

Design by Lena Skvagerson for Annie's Signature Designs

Bonus Pattern

Skill Level

◼◼☐☐ EASY

Sizes

Woman's small (medium, large, X-large, 2X-large)

Instructions are given for smallest size, with larger sizes in parentheses. When only 1 number is given, it applies to all sizes.

Finished Measurements

Chest: 37 (41, 45, 49, 53) inches

Length: 19 (20, 21, 22, 23) inches (excluding collar)

Materials

- Plymouth Yarn Encore Mega(super chunky weight; 75% acrylic/25% wool; 64 yds/100g per skein): 5 (6, 6, 7, 8) skeins navy #658

  6 SUPER BULKY
- Size 17 (12.75mm) needles or size needed to obtain gauge
- Stitch holders
- Stitch markers

Gauge

8 sts and 11 rows = 4 inches/10cm in St st.

8 sts and 15 rows = 4 inches/10cm in garter st.

To save time, take time to check gauge.

To watch a video tutorial for this project, sign in to your account at **AnniesFiction.com.**
Click on My Series in the left-hand column, then select Annie's Attic Mysteries, Special Edition.

Pattern Note

Vest is worked flat and then seamed together. Collar is then worked flat from stitches reserved along neckline.

Back

Cast on 37 (41, 45, 49, 53) sts.

Knit 12 rows.

Starting with a RS row, work in St st until piece measures 10 (10½, 11¼, 12, 12½) inches from cast-on edge, ending with a RS row.

Armhole Shaping

Row 1 (WS): K5 (5, 6, 6, 6), purl across to last 5 (5, 6, 6, 6) sts, k5 (5, 6, 6, 6).

Row 2: Knit.

Row 3: Rep Row 1.

Row 4: Bind off 2 (2, 3, 3, 3) sts, knit to end—35 (39, 42, 46, 50) sts.

Row 5: Bind off 2 (2, 3, 3, 3) sts, k3, purl across to last 3 sts, k3—33 (37, 39, 43, 47) sts.

Row 6: Knit.

Row 7: K3, purl across to last 3 sts, k3.

Rep Rows 6 and 7 until armhole measures 8 (8½, 8¾, 9, 9½) inches, ending with a WS row.

Bind off 8 (9, 10, 11, 12) sts at beg of next 2 rows.

Place rem 17 (19, 19, 21, 23) sts on holder.

Left Front

Cast on 23 (25, 27, 29, 31) sts.

Knit 12 rows.

Row 1 (RS): Knit.

Row 2 (WS): K7 (front edge), purl to end.

Rep Rows 1 and 2 until piece measures 10 (10½, 11¼, 12, 12½) inches from cast-on edge, ending with a RS row.

Armhole Shaping

Row 1 (WS): K7, purl across to last 5 (5, 6, 6, 6) sts, k5 (5, 6, 6, 6).

Row 2: Knit.

Row 3: Rep Row 1.

Row 4: Bind off 2 (2, 3, 3, 3) sts, knit to end—21 (23, 24, 26, 28) sts.

Row 5: K7, purl across to last 3 sts, k3.

Row 6: Knit.

Rep Rows 5 and 6 until armhole measures the same as back to shoulder, ending with a WS row.

Bind off 8 (9, 10, 11, 12) sts (shoulder), without working them place rem 13 (14, 14, 15, 16) sts holder.

Cut yarn.

Right Front

Cast on 23 (25, 27, 29, 31) sts.

Knit 12 rows.

Row 1 (RS): Knit.

Row 2 (WS): Purl across to last 7 sts, k7 (front edge).

Rep Rows 1 and 2 until piece measures 10 (10½, 11¼, 12, 12½) inches from cast-on edge, ending with a RS row.

Armhole Shaping

Row 1 (WS): K5 (5, 6, 6, 6), purl across to last 7 sts, k7.

Row 2: Knit.

Row 3: Rep Row 1.

Row 4: Knit.

Row 5: Bind off 2 (2, 3, 3, 3) sts, purl across to last 7 sts, k7—21 (23, 24, 26, 28) sts.

Row 6: Knit.

Row 7: K3, purl across to last 7 sts, k7.

Rep Rows 6 and 7 until armhole measures the same as back to shoulder, ending with a RS row.

Bind off first 8 (9, 10, 11, 12) sts (shoulder), purl across to last 7 sts, k7—13 (14, 14, 15, 16) sts. Leave rem sts on needle. Do not cut yarn.

Assembly

Sew shoulder seams.

Sew side seams, creating a split by starting seam after the garter st border.

Collar

With RS facing, knit across sts on right front, place back sts on LH needle from holder, knit across sts, place left front sts on LH needle from holder, and then knit to end—43 (47, 47, 51, 55) sts.

Work in garter st until collar measures 5 (5½, 6, 6½, 7) inches.

Bind off loosely.

Finishing

Weave in ends.

Block to measurements. ●

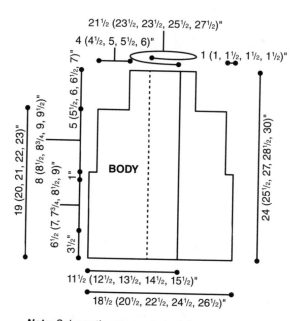

21½ (23½, 23½, 25½, 27½)"

4 (4½, 5, 5½, 6)"

7 (7)"

1 (1, 1½, 1½, 1½)"

5 (5½, 6, 6½, 7)"

8 (8½, 8¾, 9, 9½)"

19 (20, 21, 22, 23)"

6½ (7, 7¾, 8½, 9)"

1"

3½"

BODY

24 (25½, 27, 28½, 30)"

11½ (12½, 13½, 14½, 15½)"

18½ (20½, 22½, 24½, 26½)"

Note: *Schematic represents both front and back pieces after seaming with collar worked as one attached piece. Measurements are for each piece before seaming.*

KNIT STANDARD ABBREVIATIONS

approx.. approximately
beg..begin/begins/beginning
CC.. contrasting color
ch ....chain stitch
cm ....centimeter(s)
cn ....cable needle
dec(s)............................ decrease/decreases/decreasing
dpn(s)...double-point needles(s)
g..grams(s)
inc(s)...........................increase/increases/increasing
k.. knit
k2tog ....knit 2 stitches together
kfb ....knit in front and back
kwise..knitwise
LH..left hand
m .... meter(s)
MC.. main color
mm .... millimeter(s)
oz ....ounce(s)
p...purl
p2tog ....purl 2 stitches together
pat(s)... pattern(s)
pm ....place marker
psso ....pass slipped stitch over
pwise...purlwise
rem................................remain/remains/remaining
rep(s)... repeat(s)

rev St st .... reverse stockinette stitch
RH ....right hand
rnd(s)...round(s)
RS..right side
skp..slip 1 knitwise, knit 1, pass slipped stitch over—a
left-leaning decrease
sk2p.............................. slip 1 knitwise, knit 2 together,
pass slipped stitch over the stitch
from the knit-2-together decrease—
a left-leaning double decrease
sl..slip
sl 1 kwise... slip 1 knitwise
sl 1 pwise..slip 1 purlwise
sl st(s)...slip stitch(es)
ssk.. slip 2 stitches, 1 at a time,
knitwise; knit these stitches
together through the back
loops—a left-leaning decrease
st(s) ....stitch(es)
St st.................................... stockinette stitch
tbl ....through the back loop
tog ....together
WS... wrong side
wyib..................................with yarn in back
wyif................................with yarn in front
yd(s)...yard(s)
yfwd ....yarn forward
yo (yo's) .... yarn over(s)

Up to this point, we've been doing all the writing. Now it's *your* turn!

Tell us what you think about this book, the characters, the bad guy, or anything else you'd like to share with us about this series. We can't wait to hear from *you*!

Log on to give us your feedback at:
https://www.surveymonkey.com/r/CreativeWoman

Annie's® FICTION

Learn more about Annie's fiction books at

AnniesFiction.com

We've designed the website especially for you!

Access your e-books and audiobooks* • Manage your account

Choose from these great series:

Amish Inn Mysteries

Annie's Attic Mysteries

Annie's Museum Mysteries

Annie's Mystery Quilt Stitch Along

Annie's Mysteries Unraveled

Annie's Quilted Mysteries

Annie's Secrets of the Quilt

Annie's Sweet Intrigue

Antique Shop Mysteries

Chocolate Shoppe Mysteries

Creative Woman Mysteries

Hearts of Amish Country

Inn at Magnolia Harbor

Love in Lancaster County

Mistletoe Mysteries

Mysteries of Aspen Falls

Rose Cottage Book Club

Secrets of the Castleton Manor Library

Scottish Bakehouse Mysteries

Victorian Mansion Flower Shop Mysteries

THREE FORMATS FOR YOUR CONVENIENCE

HARDCOVER   E-BOOK   AUDIOBOOK*

*available in select series only

What are you waiting for? Annie's FICTION

Inn at Magnolia Harbor

Magnolia Harbor Inn

AnniesFiction.com

Enjoy Southern hospitality at its finest with sisters Grace Porter and
Charlotte Wylde, co-owners of the picturesque Magnolia Harbor Inn.
Joined by their eccentric aunt, Winnie Bennett, and their sweet shih tzu,
Grace and Charlotte have built a new life running the beautiful inn,
graciously providing a haven for those who need to get away from their
hectic lives.

In each heartwarming story of the series, you'll love getting to know the
charming residents of Magnolia Harbor, South Carolina, and the guests
who are on journeys of the heart, ready to discover important truths
about life and love during their stay.